VENERO ARMANNO

JUMPING AT THE MOON

*un*tapped

ABOUT *UNTAPPED*

Most Australian books ever written have fallen out of print and become unavailable for purchase or loan from libraries. This includes important local and national histories, biographies and memoirs, beloved children's titles, and even winners of glittering literary prizes such as the Miles Franklin Literary Award.

Supported by funding from state and territory libraries, philanthropists and the Australian Research Council, *Untapped* is identifying Australia's culturally important lost books, digitising them, and promoting them to new generations of readers. As well as providing access to lost books and a new source of revenue for their writers, the *Untapped* collaboration is supporting new research into the economic value of authors' reversion rights and book promotion by libraries, and the relationship between library lending and digital book sales. The results will feed into public policy discussions about how we can better support Australian authors, readers and culture.

See untapped.org.au for more information, including a full list of project partners and rediscovered books.

Readers are reminded that these books are products of their time. Some may contain language or reflect views that might now be found offensive or inappropriate.

To Angelina and Carmelo

CONTENTS

CONTENTS

AND THE EXCLAMATION MARKS HIT
THE PAGE !!!!!!!!!

1 Thomas Hits the Page

As he sat before his new personal computer system Thomas Petrovski had to admit that he was happy. He pressed the ON/OFF button and the error-checking triple beeps sounded the all-clear, and that made him happy. With a key here and a key there Thomas was into the word processing system, the yellow cursor blinking above the exact word in the exact sentence of the exact article he wanted, and that made him happy too.

At his right elbow were the weekend newspapers that had carried not one but two of his comprehensive film reviews *as well* as his critique of an opening in Chapel Street, that particular article appearing under the name of Tom Patterson because he lacked a little confidence in his art reviews. All, however, had been well received, but that in itself didn't make him happy— the fact that they had attracted attention most definitely made him happy.

And what attention!

The letters at his left elbow screamed for him, but Thomas only smiled as with swift keyboard fingers he continued to set the seal upon his ongoing success. This was an article about a major Australian writer, a man who, over lunch, had confessed to trading strategic information for hash during the Vietnam war. Thomas smiled at the human soul's need for absolution, and his keyboard rattled on beneath his fingers. Attention? This article would receive attention, the attention Thomas had become used to since he'd abandoned callow, turbulently meaningless journalism and success had been there to greet him.

And there was his latest success too, which made him happier still.

Thomas stood up from the computer. It had been his own little present to himself to celebrate his recent sweet success. Like a child stealing down a staircase on Christmas Eve to gaze upon the neatly wrapped gifts waiting under the tree, he now tiptoed down the corridor to his bedroom.

The door was slightly ajar. With his index finger he pushed it open. In his grand four-poster bed she lay naked, face down, and with her auburn hair across the pillow so that all he saw of her face was a glimpse of smooth cheek, the tip of her Roman nose.

She likes to sleep face down, he thought with awe.

It was four in the morning and from the doorway he watched as she lay without covers. By the indirect light of the corridor her back was taut and muscled, her bottom golden and round. He watched with greed, but then because he was an emotional man and because his emotions had been used a lot in the past week—well, at least hers had been—a tear came to his eye. Yet even as he wiped it away he was smiling. Success, sweet success, great success. Money and love and attention. Mega-success— he liked the sound of that one!

Carefully drawing the bedroom door shut he padded in his socks back to the study where the cursor blinked at the last letter of the last word he had typed. Thomas checked his wristwatch and yawned. It was late but he felt a kind of love for this new toy. Time at least for one more reassuring trot through Mr Spellcheck. He watched the screen with the same smile as had been on his face when he had watched the bottom *sans-pareil*.

An associate at lunch one day when they had drunk a bottle of champagne apiece—something French and expensive—had leaned conspiratorially toward him: 'You know why I like champagne, Thomas? There's no taste in the world like it—except for the taste of success.'

Champagne?

But *this* was the taste of success! This screen with its EGA graphics capability, its unerring image as he typed, the processor with its microtechnology and forty megabytes of formatted fun. Success was the steady beat of the cursor, the once around Mr Spellcheck, this meander through Thesaurus Gardens that Thomas couldn't resist performing. The styled keyboard so light to the touch but so precise. The texture of the keytops under his fingertips. The very look of the keys. The optional repeat mechanism on any key so that, for example, when you held the exclamation mark key down you could fill a whole page with !!!!!!!!!!!!!!!!!!!!'s if you wanted—a thousand pages! Success was features and facilities and this baby had more features and facilities than Thomas could handle in a lifetime! Success? This was excess—and loving it!

He checked his watch once more. Very late indeed. His fingers wavered over the commands which would put his work into a digital drawer and let him crawl into his warm bed. It was going on five and he was overtired now, wondering when the first light of dawn would splay the night-time clouds.

Usually Thomas worked to the strictest of schedules, breaking his writing day into two sessions: (a) 4.00 p.m.—6.00 p.m. and (b) 1.00 a.m.—3.00 a.m.

These two blocks gave him all the time he needed for his journal and newspaper articles, his letters, his sporadic fiction. Thomas could not explain how his working life had settled into those two particular session times: when pressed, like the OFF button on his EGA screen, he went blank. How could he explain that he loved, sincerely loved, those two time slots, especially the latter one, when the world was finally quiet and his thoughts gave an audible beat to the blinking of his screen's cursor.

But now it was 5 a.m. and he was tired, and within his general happiness there was a slight annoyance that the schedule he had so assiduously kept to for so long had been broken—at least since *her* arrival. He would have to put things to rights, but how could he have known that her urges for making love would come at his allocated writing times? Who could have known that once she was in the house with him her timing would be so precise? And who, at such a tender time in their relationship, would have said, 'Darling, my writing, my writing!'

Not Thomas.

After chasing his prize so mercilessly and with such diligence was he now going to ruin everything just as she was his?

Not Thomas.

Success, he knew, you *never* gave away. Success, he knew, you *always* treated respectfully.

He rubbed his eyes. The next day—today—his body clock would be out but he was determined to rise at the right time (10.30 a.m.), be at his aerobics class on time (12 noon), go to lunch with his agent and friend, Walter Jeffries (1.30 p.m. last Friday of every month), do his weight-training (2.45 p.m.—3.45 p.m. every other day), and be ready for his first writing session, sitting down, screen on, cursor blinking, by 4.00 p.m. In order there was rationality, with rationality there was purpose, and with purpose came—

Success!

She had not moved since he had looked in on her an hour before.

Oh he loved her, how he loved that small golden bottom resting on his La Galleria sheets from Paris.

The first time he had spoken to her was at the Kazachek photography exhibition—walls and walls of animal pound pets; seas of cats and dogs being put to sleep, destroyed, burned in ovens after fatal injections; piles of pet ash all that remained for recalcitrant owners to see, had they been there. All those black and white photos of animal misery and pain captured for the Artistic Statement that he was to review for the weekend papers. After the photos Thomas had expected the next room to be a showing of paintings executed in pet dog and cat blood.

Instead, there she had been, in that empty little room, sitting alone on an unvarnished coffee table while in the main gallery champagne and canapés were arriving for the *cognoscenti*.

It seemed natural to talk to that stranger, Katherine Kramer by name, married to a policeman and looking as unhappy as the animals in the gallery's photos. Later, weeks and months later, when things really started happening between her and Thomas, he found himself wondering over and over, 'But what does she want, what is it that she wants?'

Thomas now stood in the doorway of his bedroom at 5.15 a.m., Friday just before dawn, with his precious schedules blown and his eyes red from exhaustion and the radiation from his expensive computer screen, with the same question in his mind.

But he only asked himself the question now because he knew the answer. Katherine Kramer wanted *him*.

Only five mornings before this morning, in the face of the protestations, cursing, and abrupt surrender of her policeman husband, Katherine had packed a bag, walked out of the house, caught a taxi and had arrived at Thomas's home—which she knew well from their mornings and afternoons together—to stay. Thomas had been ecstatic, and now here she still lay, her golden back turned to him, asleep face down.

She likes to sleep like that, he marvelled again. My Katherine, my Kathy.

He loved the sound of her name, the cadence of it, could almost believe he had fallen not for the person, but for that name with its wonderful variations.

My Katherine, my Kathy, my Katie, Kath, Katya, Katherina. Mia cara Katherina. Katie mon amour. Mein vrinde Katherine. *My, my, my*. Katherine the Great. Soon no longer to be Mrs Katherine Kramer—what was her maiden name? Only twenty-six, married in haste and repenting at leisure. Katherine, Kate, my Katie. Celebrated by the purchase of a new personal computer system.

Thomas wanted to go to the bathroom, to brush his teeth

then finally join her in the bed, but he slumped against the door-jamb, tired but still looking down upon her sleeping form. If he had moved his eyes a little he would have seen light breaking through the clouds that had brought a little night-time rain, but he saw only money, love and attention, the best that his perfect world had to offer.

2 Daniel Doodles

When Daniel Kramer doodled, his unconscious mind liked to draw perfect circles. Leonardo da Vinci, history tells us, had the ability to draw freehand absolutely perfect circles. From the mental picture in his great artist's mind, through the trained synapses of his nervous system, out would come the geometrically exact circle. Danny Kramer had read about that once in a *Reader's Digest* left hanging on a hook in a police barracks outhouse situated west of Dubbo. That had been years back, when he had been in his late teens and was still green, but the envy that he felt in his very soul for that ability had remained with him.

Daniel Kramer was doodling now, near-perfect circles that stared him in the face from where he drew them on the misted glass of his bathroom mirror. He stood at the basin, freshly showered, hair washed, his face lathered with shaving cream and his safety razor heating in the scalding water in the basin. It was 6.15 a.m., roughly an hour after Thomas Petrovski had stood watching the near-perfect circles of Daniel's wife's bottom.

A delayed telepathy as it were: in the misted mirror Danny might have been etching an Impressionist's view of the sight that had so transfixed his rival.

As the peppermint scented lather threatened to dry over his morning beard, Daniel with his index finger drew one circle as well as he could, stepped back and contemplated it, carefully drew another next to it and contemplated it, then quickly and with anger drew a third below the first two. That one was as imperfect a circle as he had drawn since kindergarten. Then he drew a line that connected them all together.

'A triangle,' said Daniel, who hated triangles. 'A bloody triangle.'

He labelled each circle. The first was K for Katherine, the next was D for Daniel, and the third was TP—not for Thomas Petrovski but for That Prick.

'Thirty-seven years old and in a fuckin' love triangle,' he mused aloud, then angrily wiped the mirror clean of the fuckin' love triangle and attacked his face with the hot razor. When he was done blood from several nicks under his chin ran down his throat, a slight flow which looked worse because of his wet face and neck. Danny watched with grim satisfaction then gazed further down, studying his shoulders, biceps and arms, his rib cage, raised diaphragm and convex mid-section. Muscles, muscles, muscles, and at six-one he knew how to carry himself to accentuate those muscles. The sight of his muscles, muscles, muscles usually cheered him up immensely, but that morning, the sixth day of his wife's exit, his red eyes beheld no happy sight.

When he had been flatfoot Constable Kramer, then flatterfoot Senior Constable Kramer, his imposing physique had stymied most law-breakers. Now that he was Senior Constable Kramer, Computer Services Division, Computer Services Officer Grade 10, no longer a flatfoot but a shiny-bum, his great bulk intimidated only his co-workers, the secretaries, and the computer salesmen who faced his fourteen-inch biceps with unhappy smiles.

Daniel hated being a shiny-bum—he longed for the halcyon days of the flatfoot (he preferred the title used within the ranks of foot soldier)—but for Katherine and the marriage and general longevity he had enrolled himself in external Computer Awareness courses, had slogged through the long nights of assignments and study and computer consoles, and had lain awake long evenings wondering whether or not, somewhere in the philosophic distance between relational and codasyl data-bases, there was a place for him. And finally in his police department, where millions were spent on computer systems and progress was a word rarely used, there was a place for Daniel Kramer.

All for Katherine.

She had taken him nearly full-perfect circle. From those early days of bitterness as a self-hating teenager who became a cop to exert authority the way his world-hating cop-father had done all his life, all the way to a wife-loving husband and computer professional, now back into the morass of self-doubt and pity that had all along still been lurking behind his own eyes, ready to welcome him back.

He knew the Pit too well. The Pit had driven him since his early teens, day in and day out, grunting and groaning in gymnasiums, taming his terror as he abseiled down ridiculously dangerous mountainsides, stifling his pain through relentless marathons—the list was endless and legendary within the force. After his morning shave now he was off to Joe's Health and Fitness club for a good hour and a half of ironwork while his ever-softening co-workers slept on in their warm beds with their warm wives.

Police work killed marriages, that Daniel knew. As a single man and foot soldier he had seen the bust-ups of his suffering mates. Now here he was, a shiny-bum, no danger, no tension, no anxieties that any other office worker in the whole world didn't experience, and he had lost his wife anyway. If it wasn't the police work, wasn't it obvious that—?

The Pit called out to him.

As he finished up in the bathroom his temples throbbed with too many sleepless nights and the thought of having to spend another day sitting with the fat desk jockeys and computer console junkies. He had hated them and hated them more now, with their dinner parties and football and wine clubs and doting, respectful wives. All the family stuff they had to go on with—christenings, poolside barbecues, poker nights, marriages, theatre engagements, mortgages and babies' trousers and retirement funds, all with their faithful fat wives, wives, wives. Wives who had been through everything with them, wives who would never have affairs, wives who would never dream of leaving.

Just the day before at morning tea, three overstuffed, over-promoted, underachieving fellow Computer Services officers had been standing around the mineral water cooler that the benevolent Establishment had installed to cut down on staff consumption of high-caffeine-content bulk instant coffee, and in his current state Daniel had listened with disgust:

'... and the missus says, "Don' buy the fillet steak, you think we've got royalty coming?"'

'... a bottle of cold chablis, and Jenny looks at me in that certain way ...'

'... and we've had them enrolled in ballet classes of all things. Ballet classes? God! But then I see them, six and seven apiece, little blondies in their leotards, and I think—yeah.'

It had been the smugness in their faces, the tacit acceptance of their proper place in the family unit, something that was as round and perfect as da Vinci's freehand circles, that had turned up Daniel's heat. And he had simmered all day until the juice was gone and he was all black and cracked and smoking inside, and later that night he had attacked Joe's Health and Fitness club with a splendid and wild passion that had left the others staring. And inside he cooked and cooked and cooked and Katherine had still not rung. Up and down went the weights, up and down, up and down, and Katherine was with TP and the beautiful circles of iron and lead pumped in a way that would have crippled mere mortals.

Now dressed, unrefreshed by sleep, driving his 1971 EH Holden once again to Joe's Health and Fitness club, Daniel mused upon the wormdick, TP, the one who had ...

The morning, with its slight chill and damp left by the

evening rain, was absent to him. The sky and the streets were lost to his reflections, and he drove his battered car through the stops and turns to the gymnasium without conscious thought, as if the route was so ingrained in him it was part of his genetic make-up. If his body or senses longed for any stimulation, it was only for the iron, the perfect weights, the gymnasium's wide-screen mirror that showed his bulging body. His triceps and his deltoids and his latisima dorsae ached to be stretched and strained, ached for Katherine, ached for TP.

Especially galling was to have to think about TP while driving through the early morning streets in his old Holden.

A few days after Katherine had made things clear to him, Daniel had sought to make things clearer for himself. Call it Police Training That Never Dies. With accumulated work time off in lieu, Danny had spied on TP, watched him in a sweater and tracksuit pants pruning his rosebushes, trimming the negligible weeds from his front flowerbeds while Gershwin had played loudly from inside the house. Daniel had continued to watch TP's house when TP himself had retired inside and not emerged for an hour, then later had followed TP's silver Lancia to an upmarket city gymnasium.

So TP cared how his buns looked! All the revelations of the day were as meaningful to Danny as the word of the New Testament is to the devout.

And then—what a day he had picked to follow his enemy!—the silver Lancia had gone from the upmarket gymnasium to a prestige caryard. Daniel watched from across the street as TP, now wearing designer casuals, shook the hand of a stern-faced salesman and took delivery—that very day!—of a red Fiat Pininfarina Spyder with webbed mags, new Pirelli tyres, and a cream-coloured convertible top. And not an early model either, it had been at least an '83 or '84. Rare as hen's teeth and more beautiful than anything Daniel had ever touched in his life.

The red Spyder joined the great throng of traffic in the road but Daniel—who had loved convertible sportscars for years, but necessarily from afar—had remained in his own car with his hands gripping the steering wheel, deflated, depressed, defeated.

David remembered these things as he arrived at 7.15 a.m., Joe of Joe's Health and Fitness club saying to him, 'Danny my boy pump them up, pump them up!'

It all came and went that morning, Joe's locker room camaraderie, the weights, bicycle and mirror, the hot shower afterwards, the drive to the police Central Computer Services branch car park where an ageing attendant took care of his Holden for him—as if anyone would covet it!

Coffee, a meeting, his terminal and keyboard, a report to be written that was interrupted by the arrival of a computer salesman with halitosis, all came and went and it was 10.30 a.m. and the wormdicks were around the water cooler again. Their talk, their tone, brought him back to reality with a thudding sense of hatred while the tea assistant's trolley clattered by his steel government-issue desk.

In his anger he almost went to them; instead, with a strong and steady hand he drew his telephone to him, cradled it in his ample arms and chest as tenderly as if it had been a baby. As well as everything else, he knew TP's unlisted telephone number—call it Police Contacts That Never Die.

Daniel now doodles as the telephone rings away in TP's home. He draws circles that would do da Vinci proud, but these circles, this morning, all interconnect. The telephone rings on and on, the wormdicks discuss their wives and their families from around the water cooler. Without wife or family, Daniel stares down at his perfect picture of what his perfect world has become.

3 Excuse Me!

Excuse me, excuse me ... look, can you hear me? I really am sorry to interrupt all this but really—the most terrible thing!

It's just after 10.30 a.m. and I've just put the phone down from Danny. Tommy's still asleep of course. When you don't work you don't have to get out of your bed, other than to fix tea and a sandwich of course.

Listen to me, that sounds really nasty, doesn't it? Look, I'm not a nasty person or anything like that, it's just that Tommy ... well—what can I say? It's only been six days and—

No talking out of court, right?

Okay, so Daniel's just rung and he wants to see me after he finishes work, for a coffee and to get a few things off his chest. Of course he does. Sometimes I can't believe what I've done, to him, to myself. Most of all to him, I guess. Guilt is something that's easy for me to understand, but let's not get too sentimental. He wants to see me. God, I want to see him. Five-thirty then, at the coffee shop in town. I know there's a thousand coffee shops in town, but I know which one he means. When you've been married to someone for so many years and all that.

But here's where I come into this.

I put down the phone, and by the armchair on the filthy carpet of this, Tommy's filthy flat, I find a story he's writing. Some people have jobs and responsibilities, but Tommy, my love, he collects the dole and writes stories that nobody wants to read. Much less me. But I pick this one up because I don't want to think about either Daniel or Tommy for a while. And what do I find? Thomas and Daniel and some bimbo called Katherine Kramer.

Well excuse me!

Right, my name is Katherine Kramer. Right! I'm married to Daniel Kramer, yes he's a cop but I can tell you he's no Arnie Schwarzenegger lookalike, and six days ago I packed up and left him. So you think it's pretty awful that I left him for another man? Well, that's your problem. Okay, mine too. I think it's bloody sordid. I left Daniel and moved straight in with Tommy. Not Thomas Petrovski, but Tommy Patterson, yes, the name that this Petrovski writes his 'art reviews' under because he still 'lacks a little confidence' in them. I mean to say, who does Tommy think he's kidding?

Let's get some facts straight.

Thomas Petrovski is a figment of my Tommy's infertile imagination. He's put us and our situation into a story! The gall of the man. And what an exercise in self-aggrandisement! All that about success, attention and love. And money. And Katherine Kramer's golden bottom sticking up in the air from his imported Parisian sheets. He's obsessed! I work out a little with an aerobics class but I can tell you my backside doesn't look too much like the perfect circles Daniel-the-Goliath is supposed to draw. If only!

Well, I guess that's the key—if only. Tommy probably dreamt this fantasy up out of, 'If only I was rich, if only I could get published.'

If only I could get my hands on him!

I know I shouldn't knock him, it's just a shock to read about yourself and your husband and your lover in a story that takes so much dramatic licence. And written by someone you're supposedly close to. Is nothing sacred?

I met Tommy in a supermarket. God knows I've never been to an art gallery opening. We started talking at the checkout, then the following week I noticed him there again. And the week after. Gets me thinking he's hanging around for me—which he was. Well, talk about flattering. Daniel and I, we don't live in the best part of town, you know. Around here a housewife gets flattered about once a decade, but here was this cute fellow looking out for me from week to week. Don't get me wrong, I wasn't hanging around for anything. I love Daniel, he may be as dull as dog-meat sometimes, but I love him. It's just that, well, you probably get the picture.

And when Tommy and I got together, he wanted it all so badly I couldn't believe it. He *was* obsessed! I'd never been so desired in all my life. He wanted me every day, every hour. Of course I couldn't believe it, and although I was sick at what I was doing to Danny, a part of me was so thrilled that I just ran away with it all. And after the mornings and afternoons in Tommy's flat I knew I couldn't stay with my marriage any more.

So here's this story Tommy's writing for heaven knows what reason. He's up to the part where Daniel rings. And Daniel did ring, at the right time too. Kinda creepy if you think about it. Bloody writers!

I like Petrovski the best. Oh the gall! The letters of offer he keeps talking about, the articles and the attention! When Tommy writes the only letters at his left elbow would be the ones about rental arrears and 'please explain'. He's thirty years of age and hasn't worked, except for oddjobs, since he was twenty-one. Hasn't had a girlfriend either, except for me, since he was twenty-one! Where's he been all that time? On a government employment service file, that's where, with his head in fantasy land. I like the Fiat convertible too. Tommy, poor guy, drives the 1971 EH Holden Daniel's supposed to hobble around in. Pirellis! The tyres of Tommy's car are so bald he's afraid to drive down the road for his nightly Big Mac and fries! Petrovski's got commitments, schedules, an expensive word processor. Tommy's got a typewriter his sister handed down to him, and on the wrong weeks he can't buy a new ribbon for it.

Oh, Tommy, I love you, you great thickhead.

And Daniel. Mr Responsibility himself. He's in the force, that part's true, and in the computer branch. Never been a foot soldier that I know of, but he carries around the obligatory policeman's beer belly. Tommy's gonna have one too if he's not careful. The only thing that scares him is that he just hasn't got the money to drink all the beer he'd like to.

You should have heard Daniel's voice on the phone. He wants to see me, yes, and I want to see him. I can't deny it. For the past three or four years he's been urging me to get off the pill. He wants a kid. He wants to shoulder more responsibility, and let me tell you, he'd be smiling while taking it. He wants more than one kid—he wants a colony of them. He wants the family life that he missed out on. Oh Tommy got a little of that right, but hatred? A morass of pity?

Not Daniel, never Daniel. He would be there for you anytime you needed him. Your problems would become his problems if that would help you out. Hate? I don't think he even hates me for what I've done. This planet wasn't meant for people like him. But after all that, he's as exciting as sponge cake. Tommy's story is wrong, all wrong.

I like the Katherine Kramer in his story too—the bimbo with the bum everyone seems to have on the brain. That's the most telling part of the story, if you ask me, the most telling part about Tommy the writer too. This woman that Petrovski's in love with, what do we learn about her? What do we know about her character, what does Petrovski know of her soul? Nothing! He's in love with a human being that is no more than a well-developed arse! Her contribution to the plot is to lie asleep in the raw and be gloated over! Thanks a lot, Tommy! When do you get on to the perky, champagne-glass tits? What about the slender thighs and their silken touch? Thanks a million!

So this Petrovski, what's he in love with?

And Tommy, what's he in love with?

Maybe I'm being too bitter, maybe I'm expecting too much, maybe this story is just Tommy's dreams on paper. Can you knock him for that? We all have to dream, we all want an adventure—don't I know it!—or a great romance. There's an old song Tommy plays on the stereo every now and then, I bet he was thinking of these lines as his pen hit the page:

> Imagine a past that you wished you had lived
> Full of heroes and villains and foes.

You can see where Tommy's story is going, of course. Here's the set-up: the successful, methodical, ever-so-slightly arrogant Thomas: Daniel, the frustrated urban foot soldier pushed to his emotional limits; Katherine—the question mark. Well, I can see the heroism and daring just itching to be written into the pages of Tommy's notebook. And romance, and a finale with Katherine tied to the tracks with the Southern Aurora bearing down and Daniel with his mighty forearm around the throat of Thomas the Magnificent. Superman and Batman be damned. Thomas must turn the tables. Thomas will!

Excuse me!

Well, this Katherine Kramer, what if she were to throw a spanner in the works? What would that do to Tommy's little exercise in self-affection? She of the glistening back and the perfect posterior, what if she isn't happy with the way things are? What if she has a brain and she suddenly decides to use it? What if she wakes up from those Parisian sheets to the horror of what she has done to the man she loves? What if she decides ...

The sound of movement in the corridor makes me turn around abruptly, the pages of his story held in my guilty hands. Oh, he's finally awake! The darling of the dole queue, the Casanova of the computer console!

He stands in the corridor with a torn bath towel wrapped around his soft belly. His hair is tousled and he looks every inch of his thirty dissolute years. What can I say? Give him time, he scrubs up well.

—Is that my story you're holding? he asks with a yawn.

—I hope you don't mind ... It was just lying there.

—Na, na. 's fine, he says coming over and kissing me with his morning breath. Want coffee? Who was on the bloody phone so early in the morning? Jesus, some people.

—That was Daniel.

—Who!

—Daniel.

—Wha' the fuck's he want?

—He wants to meet me this afternoon, about five-thirty. For coffee. He says he wants to talk.

—You're not going!

—Tommy, I want to go back to him.

That stops him dead, and he just looks at me with those bleary eyes of his. When he's really awake, shaved, showered, dressed, and after he's had some breakfast, those eyes of his will be clear and handsome and unforgiving. Could I fight him then? I wonder. But now—

One of us has to say something. I don't know what, I don't know who. But Katherine Kramer has opened her mouth and has used her brain. But it sounds so shabby! I want to go back to him. But God help me, I mean it. Oh Daniel.

And so, finally, it's Tommy who speaks. Or it's Tommy the writer who actually speaks, because when he says, Well, I guess this changes everything, he's not looking at me. He's looking at the pages in my hands, the swine, at his *story*. I hate him.

You bet. This changes everything!

4 Thomas Hits the Page Again

With a cup of hot tea to sustain him, Thomas leaned back into his comfortable leather chair and faced the computer screen. It was just after five-thirty in the afternoon and as his schedule dictated, he'd been hard at the keyboard for an hour and a half. He was glad to be back into his routine. He'd seen Katherine off just fifteen minutes earlier, a mild interruption to his schedule, but one that he had used to brew the cup of Earl Grey that steamed at his left elbow, above his letters of offer. Thomas was smiling. Daniel had rung the house during the morning. Katherine had answered the telephone for he had still been asleep, what with the late hour of his previous night's work and all. The call, however, had roused him from his grand four-poster and just as Katherine had put the receiver down Thomas had been standing there, barefoot and tousle-haired, but wearing his white bathrobe with the letters 'TP' embroidered on the left breast.

'Who was that, darling?'

'Daniel. He wants me to meet him when he finishes work, for a cup of coffee.'

'Is that a good idea?'

'Maybe we'll have tea.'

'You know what I mean.'

'He has things to get off his chest, Thomas, that's all. And there are things we should talk about. Arrangements we should make.'

He had taken her by the shoulders then, had stared levelly into her eyes.

'Katherine, is this going to affect you and me?'

'No, Thomas. I love you.'

'Well! I'll give you a lift when you have to go,' he had said, feeling light-hearted, thinking that a run into town with Katherine in the Spyder with the top down would be fun.

Thomas had then gone into the kitchen to make some eggs, yet somehow they had ended up in the bedroom. Later, in the early afternoon, somehow they had ended up back in the bedroom again.

'Oh Thomas.' Katherine's sigh remained in his mind.

Now, cheerfully, while Katherine was off for coffee—they had decided it would be best if she took a taxi into town—a few commands had his current pet project up on the screen. It had been a hot day but the open doors and windows let the afternoon breeze drift through the house.

Of all his writing, Thomas found this type the most fun. As well as the newspaper articles and reviews, and his serious fiction, Thomas also wrote romance novels under the pseudonym of Bernadette O'Meagher. An elderly aunt had given him the idea two years earlier when he had been hard pressed for cash. So he had sent away to the publishers and all the guff had been sent back to him by return mail; perusing their information, the stories the publishers required, the approach and the pacing they looked for, and especially how much was paid to the successful author, Thomas had immediately known he was onto a winner. Soon they had accepted two of his—her—manuscripts, each of which had taken him an easy month to write. And the cheques had come, also by return post!

With the successes of *The Angel of Passion* and *Random Hearts,* Bernadette O'Meagher found it easy to interest her publishers in a trilogy, namely, *Love's Hard Promise, Love's Hard Passion,* and *Love's Hard Ride.*

Thomas/Bernadette was now into the last chapters of the final instalment. But there was a Hard Choice to make—would this really be the final instalment? Why kill a winner! Thomas/Bernadette scratched his/her head. A Hard Choice indeed. There already existed a plan for a fourth volume, titled, naturally enough, *Love's Hard Choice.*

The decision now: do away with either young Lady Sarah or young Lord Winthrup, the unknown seventh Earl of Colchester, or let them live, albeit apart, so that they might come together in a fourth book.

Either way, Thomas really wanted his readers howling into their lace handkerchiefs by the end of the current instalment. What to do?

As he/she drummed his/her fingers against the side of the keyboard, Thomas idly thought of Katherine meeting Daniel in town. She would be there at the coffee shop by now, they might just be ordering their cafe au laits or their Brazilian blends, maybe a piece of wholemeal fruitcake. Would Daniel have something sweet, something creamy and gooey? Thomas thought not. Not with that physique to look after. He had seen him once at a party, had been taken aback by the size of him, had wryly thought, 'God, the husband. Why does it have to be such a cliché? Why does he have to be so big!'

Forget about all that.

Now Bernadette O'Meagher, what of Lady Sarah? The current chapter, so close to the end of the book, had to end with a cliff-hanger. He/she/they stared hard at the screen, then, inspired, typed, 'Oh my love, what am I to do if you leave me forever?'

Thomas smiled. Heady stuff!

Then thought, *Oh my Katherine, what am I to do if you leave me forever?*

And then, because he was a *writer* and knew that it was his job to empathise with all his characters, from Daniel's point of view he thought,

Oh my wife, what am I to do now that you have left me forever?

Thomas finished his tea and shook his head respectfully. Turgid stuff, but it's a living. No need to get morbid. He pressed the command for multiple single key strikes, preparing to underline the bottom of the page to signify the end of the chapter.

The telephone's sudden loud ring within the confines of his study made him jump. He usually disconnected it whenever he was writing, but in his excitement at being back into his schedules, he had forgotten. Let it ring, he told himself. Whoever you are, bugger off. But the ringing went on and on. Damn it!

'Thomas,' Katherine's voice enquired. 'Has Daniel rung by any chance?'

Thomas was annoyed at the intrusion, even if it was Katherine. 'No!' he tried to say pleasantly, failing.

'It's just that I've been waiting here and he hasn't turned up yet.'

'Give him time. They've probably got him arresting some thirteen-year-old computer hacker.' Thomas grinned at his own witticism.

'But Daniel's always so punctual.'

So punctual? So what! Probably ejaculates to schedule, he unkindly thought, forgetting his own predilection for schedules. Guy's dull as dog-meat.

'Want me to come and get you?' he asked without enthusiasm. There was young Lord Winthrup's potential demise to consider—

'No, I'll give him a little more time. Bye, darling.'

'Au revoir, mon cherub,' he laughed down the line. Now, Winthrup, you pasty-faced limey prick, I think you will get the flick—in a nasty sort o' way, know what I mean?

Thomas still had to underline the last page of the finished chapter. His fingers hovered above the keyboard.

Well, punctual, boring Daniel Kramer, eh? Leaving Katherine to wait in some dingy coffee shop. Thomas's mind wandered. What was Daniel doing? What was Daniel thinking? To leave her waiting in those tense circumstances—punctual, boring and inconsiderate! How could someone so obsessed with his own body consider someone else's feeling? The guy was a joke with his muscle-love and gymnasiums and thrill-seeking. He was probably one of *those* deep down. Probably not so deep down!

Poor Katherine, kept waiting.

Wouldn't it be funny, Thomas thought, if Daniel wasn't going to meet her at all? What if he had only wanted to get her out of the house? He of course knew that Daniel had one day spied upon him, he'd seen him from the outset. What a cop the muscle-jerk must have been! So Thomas had lorded it up for the spy's benefit. Gershwin so loud it had nearly blown the roof off the house. *Rhapsody in Blue!* Take that, you sitting there in your rusty Holden! And then an inspired decision—go and pick up the Fiat Pininfarina Spyder he was buying, pick it up now, forget the paint-job he had booked it in for and had been waiting for. Suck on that, Daniel! I'm gonna take your wife driving in that red convertible on the sunny days that you're stuck in your lousy air-conditioned office. Spying on me, you muscle-pump! Me!

The afternoon breeze was quiet and soothing, drying the slight perspiration that had broken out on Thomas's forehead. The French doors of the house were wide open to the breeze, the windows too. Beautiful breezy airy old colonial. His study was at the side of the house and caught the best part of the afternoon cool, opening onto the veranda that went right around the old place, from the front steps to the high rear deck. What a place. Wonder what the poor people are doing! How's it feel, Daniel? Here we've got everything open and airy and cool—'s a bit hot around your side of town, isn't it? In the rental-arrears suburbs, I mean!

Now again, young Lord Winthrup, the romantic lead, the unknown seventh Earl of Colchester. Still, Thomas's hands wavered. The multiple-strike command waited for him to do the underlining. Well?

What was it—something he had eaten? Mild unease in the stomach. Well? Up on the screen the words faced him:

> Oh my love, what am I to do if you leave me forever.
> Lady Sarah?
> Young Lord Winthrup?
> Love's Hard Ride?

But there was someone on the veranda at the front of the house!

Oh my wife, what am I to do now that you have left me forever?
Shit!

Hard, heavy footsteps came around the veranda. Thomas swivelled his luxurious leather chair, turned his eyes from the screen's blinking cursor. Slow footsteps were loud to his ears.

It can't be Katherine, he told himself. Not unless she's put on a lot of weight! Then maybe it's—

Without getting up from the chair Thomas craned his neck. In a moment there was the muscle-jerk himself, framed within the French doors of Thomas's study, standing on the veranda watching him.

Thomas's mind went spinning. Thoughts like:

'I mean, why's he got to be so big?'
'Jesus, what a cliché this is!'
'Katherine waiting in the coffee shop ...'

then, as he saw the gaping maw of the police-issue

gun's muzzle, 'Police-issue? Police-issue? I can't know it's a police-issue!'

'A gun! Jesus! A gun! Jesus!' and finally,

'A cliché—it's all a cliché!'

Thomas started to say 'Daniel' but it came out 'Katherine' and in response there was an instant of thunder and an instant of overwhelming relief at not being shot, but the crimson spread across his shirt and the sense of the overwhelming nature of things would not go away. With disbelief, Thomas slumped down sideways towards his expensive personal computer, down, down, down to the sea of keys floating in the keyboard. His cheek slid down the cold face of the expensive EGA graphics screen, down he went, his nose pointing the way to the keyboard until there he came to rest, the tip of his nose pushed above the exclamation mark key.

Daniel lowered his .38. Been a long time since he rock 'n' rolled with that sucker. His hand started to shake but he was filled with a wild enthusiasm for what he had just done. Enthusiasm? Elation! Everything would be fine now. Bye, Thomas Petrifiozkey, or whoever you are! You don't look so flash now! Katherine!

Daniel looked from Thomas to the waiting computer screen. He saw the cursor blinking, also waiting. Hmm, expensive piece that one. Blast it too! Nah ... Foot soldiers never waste good fire-power, first rule.

He pocketed the hot .38 and took his leave.

Up on the screen, the words 'Oh my love, what am I to do if you leave me forever' were suddenly followed by exclamation marks.

Thomas's body stayed there, the exclamation mark key held down by his nose, and, just as he had in life loved to do, the exclamation marks hit the page!!!!!!!!!!!!!!!!!!!!

TABBY

As bad luck would have it, the day Henry Gill had been look-ing forward to for the best part of twenty years coincided with a summons to the city of Canberra to attend a cocktail party, the celebration of young Peter Stafford's rise to the Shadow Front Bench. Young Peter Stafford's ascension had been en-abled by the Shadow defence minister's demise, which had come about under the wheels of a tractor on which he had been tilling his tomato paddocks. A thick root protruding from the dirt causing the Shadow minister to stop his tractor and take hold of his mattock, a badly serviced handbrake, a slight decline in the contours of the land—thus is the great-ness of others born, Henry Gill told himself during his flight to the city.

And because of all this, he also mused, a third gin and tonic fortifying him, he was missing out on this great day, the day of his last child's departure from home. That seventeen-year-old girl of his with the dancer's legs and the rock singer's husky voice, the last of the Gill offspring, would be bundled by his wife onto the Inter-State Express bound for Mittagong, where her boyfriend—Max the Potter—lived, and where she must now live because she was so totally, so overwhelmingly in love with him. At seventeen! Henry Gill tried to catch the attention of the stewardess for another gin. Seventeen!

In spite of all this, however, in spite of the sad means by which his long-lost freedom had returned to him, Henry felt a sense of elation that was more than simply the effects of a few good drinks. After twenty years, free at last from the little peo-ple he had brought into the world, free from the direct encum-brance of parenthood, free to do whatever he wanted whenever he wanted with whomever he wanted. Well, mainly his wife, of course, mainly his wife.

The run of the house was now his again, the television was his, the sound system, the lounge room and the dining room, the wine cellar. No more pick-ups after late classes, no more drop-offs to Saturday sports, no more P&C meetings, no more approving pats on the head and certainly no more of the stern lectures he had always been so embarrassed to give. The last of the Gill brood was out into the world and the mornings and nights were his to spend in any way he pleased.

Or to put it more correctly, all of it was *theirs* once more. But they had never discussed this day that meant so much to Henry Gill—what would the wife of Henry Gill feel now that they were to be alone together in the great house, just as in their early orgiastic days of marriage?

After the flight had arrived safely and he was settled into his hotel room, feeling both happy and sad, Henry Gill rang home. The cocktail party preceded a black tie dinner that was to be held in the grand ballroom of Parliament House, so Henry was dressed in his formal black suit as he dialled his home number. The hotel valet had not returned with the black leather shoes he had sent off for polishing and the air-conditioning was, as always, set too high. Even in his socks his feet were cold. As he waited for his wife to answer the telephone he watched the hangnail of his big toe poking out through a hole in his black silk sock.

'She was so happy, Henry, I don't think she'll miss us at all.'

'She'll miss us,' he said with the beginnings of a tear in his eye. 'But she's supposed to be happy too. That's what this is all about.'

'If only you could have been at the station.'

'I know, I know,' he replied, his tone bearing the cruel weight of his office. 'But don't you worry about her. Henry Jr and Sammy both started out like this, and they turned out okay.'

'I miss her already, Henry.'

'We missed Henry Jnr and Sammy too. But it'll be okay. Don't worry about her—she'll ring as soon as she gets to Mittagong.' He shuddered as he thought of the welcome which awaited her—Max the Potter, with that beard and those hands that looked so much like a product of his kiln. 'I'll be back by tomorrow night. The nine-twenty. Meet me at the airport?'

And Mrs Henry Gill had cried then. In light of her reaction to their daughter's exit from the home, Henry was glad he had never spoken about his own feelings. Freedom indeed! He would have to coax Mrs Gill into enjoying their new situation. His mind was filled with the memories of their early days, before the kids came along, the whiskies in bed, the late nights, sex in the morning, afternoon and evening. Lovemaking in the little Ford Prefect he used to drive in his university days. The secluded beaches they sometimes took advantage of. But the home, the home ... Henry sat on the side of his hotel room's hard bed, and as he waited for his polished shoes he remembered the things he and his new wife used to do within the sanctity of their home. And now again. He was still young—fifty was nothing for a politician! And his wife—

There was a tap on his door and when he opened it there his shoes waited, side by side on the hotel's drekky carpet, as if they had walked there themselves. The hotel had a no tipping policy so the staff didn't like to linger. Henry pulled on his shoes and straightened his bow-tie, glad at the interruption to his thoughts. At that juncture he didn't want to have to think about the passage of years, his wife and his new freedom, at least not all in the same breath.

At the cocktail party and during the formal dinner to commemorate God knows what great ancient event in the Party's history, Henry drank too much. If someone had been unkind enough to ask him if he was celebrating something or drowning some particular sorrow, he would have replied, 'I don't know. For the love of heaven, I just don't know.'

The port was being served and the speeches went on and

on. At least it was good port, something mellow, but Henry had trouble reading the label. He fumbled with his glasses but still could not quite make out the label. Good port anyway, he mumbled to his neighbour, his mind not on the port or the speeches, but on his daughter somewhere on her way into the bearded ceramicist's hard hands. He thought of them together, could see them kissing and lying together, and the image became him and his wife as they had been in the early days—bed, bed, kitchen floor, bed. Fresh orange juice in the morning and cheap champagne at night.

He quickly finished off the expensive port and when his turn came Henry was again glad to abandon his thoughts. Before the crowd in their expensive black suits and silk ties, Henry's oratory was precise and full of barely restrained rage at the government's recent range of financial fiascos. The port hadn't diminished his capacity for performance, and he rammed his speechwriter's points home to the collective applause and approval of his peers.

He could tell what the other Shadow ministers and Shadow underlings would be thinking, that there was still fire and rage and purpose in the fifty-year-old belly of Henry Gill. The true politician's gifts: potency and passion!

Fresh orange juice in the morning, cheap champagne at night. Henry took his leave of the podium, sweating profusely, soaking up the applause. Fresh orange juice in the morning ...

'Henry! Fabulous stuff! Wonderful speech!' the new Shadow bod for defence enthused as Henry walked past his table. Peter Stafford took Henry's arm and dragged himself up out of his seat, nearly toppling Henry in the process. Finally they stood together, sweating face to sweating face, the younger man hopelessly obese and twice Henry's size. 'What a night, what do you think? What a night! You know, I'm not the type of guy who goes in for this type of stuff. I'm a quieter sort of guy. But what a night!'

'Quite a night,' Henry agreed, and they beamed at each other with the camaraderie of success, champagne, and port.

'You know, Henry,' Stafford leaned closer, 'we should head up to the International—just you and me. Get ourselves some Moët et Chandon and a couple of gels. Remember the Wrest Point conference? Just you and me again, what say you, Henry?'

Henry grinned at the memory of the Wrest Point conference. The courtesy room just off from the casino, the free drinks laid on at the end of proceedings, the girls Peter Stafford had succeeded in arranging.

'All on plastic,' Henry whispered.

'Of course—American Express. Gold card!'

They laughed and held each other with the memory of the good times; however a part of Henry Gill was becoming more and more detached from the idea of 'a couple of gels'. He stared into the cherubic face which held so much promise of more good times to come, and felt a coldness rise up through his well-polished leather shoes.

Stafford was not so drunk that he didn't notice. 'Henry? What's the matter? You've gone white as a—What, old son? Post-dinner port upset the belly?' he asked, attempting humour and not succeeding. He really wanted to move on.

'Do you hear that, Peter?'

'Hear what?'

'Must be a plague of cats in Canberra. Just listen to them outside.'

'What!' Stafford stared at Henry's pasty-white face and felt a moment of panic. Was Henry going to have some sort of attack, right here, on this great night? 'Henry, I'd call it a day if I were you. Listen, this guy here'll get you a taxi.' He motioned desperately for a waiter but none came. 'Henry ...'

'Listen to them,' Henry spoke in a normal voice. 'Bloody horrible things.'

'Henry,' Stafford repeated. 'Henry, maybe you should get on home—What do you say?'

A couple of *gels*, the crying of cats, fresh orange juice in the morning and cheap champagne at night. The coldness that came up through his polished Italian shoes.

Henry drew a deep breath. 'Got papers, Peter,' he lied. 'Up in the room. Have to get into them tonight or there'll be hell to pay. Love to come with you but—' He spread his hands and smiled, then wandered off. Peter Stafford watched as Henry left the grand ballroom, and felt a mild sense of relief. If there was some sort of a problem, it had nothing to do with him. Now at last—the International and his gold card!

As for Henry Gill, a red taxi from the fleet that waited in front of the House took him back to his hotel. Once in his room he fixed himself a nightcap, took off the stifling monkey-suit, and sat in his boxer shorts watching the video station of the television. Everyone in Opposition was wearing boxer shorts these days, ever since the Leader had distributed an article from *Scientific American* that discussed the testicular dangers of wearing what Australians take as ordinary men's underwear. That was the Leader for you, Henry thought as he swilled the ice in his whisky, all good Party men must be kept whole to perpetuate the Party race.

Talk about forward planning!

On the video channel, a gratuitous sex act was taking place. Henry watched without interest, feeling none of the usual stirrings from within his boxer shorts.

'Shouldn't drink so damn much,' he told himself, shivering with the air-conditioning. He put himself under the covers of the bed and toyed with the idea of ringing for a girl. It would take less than half an hour for one to arrive, and he had any choice of plastic to pay with. Yet, again, he felt a curious sense of detachment, and instead thought about his daughter.

'Mixed drinks and mixed emotions,' he told himself as he reached over to the bedside controls and switched the picture on the television screen off.

In a moment he was drifting into sleep and in doing so heard, or thought he heard, the crying of a cat—it seemed so close it might have been in the executive suite with him.

The sound disturbed Henry Gill more than he realised. His sleep was full of dreams of a tawny tabby that sat at the foot of the bed, its sharp little teeth gnawing patiently through the skin and muscle of his left foot's big toe, its sandpaper tongue lapping and scraping at his tiny bonework.

The next day, at intervals of roughly ten to fifteen minutes, Henry Gill made sure that the big toe of his left foot was intact. It occupied his day and possessed his poor hungover mind. In the twelve-seater with its wing-mounted props and indifferent servings of tomato juice, crackers and cheese, he reflected on—alternately—his big toe and tawny cats. Henry shivered with disgust at the memory of what the tabby had been doing to him.

At home, after dinner and a martini, Mrs Henry Gill gave him a warm bath with salts, dried him off with a soft towel, powdered his parts for him and took him into the bedroom. In the semi-dark, his mind muffled by the morbidity of his hangover, Henry Gill and Mrs Henry Gill found that he couldn't take advantage of their new household freedom—of course, his toe and that awful cat!

Mrs Gill held him close and spoke her soothing and understanding words, but then, adding insult to injury, Henry Gill heard the family tabby whining away downstairs.

'What the hell is that?'

'Poor Tommykins, I haven't fed him. He's outside the front door.'

'Let him stay there.'

'Oh Henry. I'll go and feed him.'

'No!' Henry suddenly shouted. 'I'll go!'

'All right!'

He pushed himself from the bed—anything to get away from this moment of masculine embarrassment—and went down the carpeted stairs in his bare feet. What a hangover! Henry felt detached from the bedroom, from the lips of his wife, just as the previous evening—

But there was no feeling at all—not even the ghost of a feeling!

'Even a man who loses his arm,' he mused as he entered the kitchen and switched on the light, 'remembers what it was like to have an arm. Sometimes he even feels as if it's *still* there.'

He knew this as a fact—another article from *Scientific American* that the Leader had distributed, that one for purposes unknown.

'But me—' he considered within the privacy of the large and expensive kitchen, but the thought trailed off.

The cat whined behind the front door of the house and, with distaste, Henry let it come in. He touched the warm fur with the back of his hand, then the creature pranced straight to the kitchen with Henry following.

'Open this yourself,' he whispered down to the ageing family pet. The Chicken 'n' Liver smelt like offal. Tommykins rumbled and purred around Henry's ankles, tried to jump up onto the kitchen counter, stretched one paw up high, which Henry hit at with the can-opener. He found some old newspaper and spread it carefully on the cork-tile floor, then Tommykins was served dinner in a yellow plastic bowl.

Henry stood in his pale-blue dressing gown, the kitchen's fluorescent light both stark and overbright. He was watching his pet as it snuffled greedily in its bowl. Of course it was greedy for the food, what other physical pleasures did it have to look forward to? Henry felt he had never really looked at this thing that lapped saucers of milk, ate foul meat out of a can, and pushed its way into his lap when he sat watching current affairs programs for news of his department's press releases. Look at that awful grey furry neutered creature, with its thin tail sticking up in a question mark and its puckered anus staring blindly back at him. Disgusting asexual creature—a nought, a nothing, a big fat zero!

Henry thought of his innocent big toe, the one on his left foot. Damn!

Before he quite understood what he was doing, the meat tenderiser from the kitchen cabinet, third drawer down on the right, was in his hand and had swung in a wide arc that went right across the fluorescent tube and ended in a thump.

'Is everything all right, Henry?' Mrs Gill called from their bedroom back up the stairs.

'Of course, darling, of course! Dropped something!'

On Tommykins' head! Henry laughed to himself.

But soon he stood with the meat tenderiser in his guilty hand and the fingers of his other hand stuffed into his dry mouth. He stared down at his handiwork for long minutes, his eyes huge and round, then quickly Henry rummaged through the kitchen drawers for the tough green garbage bags he knew Mrs Gill to favour in her weekly grocery shopping.

The months of November and December were quiet times for Henry Gill and his political associates. In those weeks before Christmas no one wanted to hear about the Government, much less the Opposition parties, so, politically, Henry was limited to making calls or taking calls, throwing darts at the dartboard installed in his small office, and very occasionally travelling to Sydney and Canberra. Whenever he did he avoided young Peter Stafford, for no other reason than that he reminded Henry of a fat neutered cat, even with his penchant for Moët et Chandon and 'gels'.

Henry Gill avoided Mrs Henry Gill too, thoughts of conjugal freedom no longer anywhere within hearing distance of his conscious mind.

For her part, Mrs Gill spent the months of her husband's political vacuum vainly praying that little Tommykins would one day reappear at their doorstep. For her, isolation was almost complete. The twins, Henry Jr and Sammy, had moved away two years earlier, then the daughter had gone, and—almost on the same day—Tommykins had also disappeared. The final link in Mrs Gill's chain of loneliness was Henry himself, and his bedroom reticence.

This forced Mrs Henry Gill to find other pursuits. She discovered competition bridge, in the process also discovering that her analytical mind made her a popular partner. Through her bridge group, there came an invitation for her to attend a local women writers meeting. There, her outspoken views on the current political milieu so impressed the others that they encouraged her to put onto paper some of the points she could make so forcefully—twenty years of marriage had certainly had an effect! The result was a one act play that Mrs Henry Gill herself performed for the members and friends of the group.

She wrote a letter to her daughter, who was now in Sydney, no longer in love with the calloused hands of Max but with the voice of a singer in a three-piece Thrash band, the motto of the band being *Three Nights. Three Lives. Three Chords.*

In her letter, Mrs Gill wrote: 'Even in suburbia, darling, there are things which must be sought after with determination, things to be discovered, things which can help one discover one's true potential.'

And in Sydney, reading these lines, the daughter of Mr and Mrs Henry Gill assumed—with a breaking heart—that her mother had finally taken a lover.

But back to Henry. During those months his life was quiet and relatively inactive. At night he listened for the yowling of the neighbourhood cats, and always their gut-wrenching cries came at the times when he felt the most despair at his place in the world. His dreams were haunted by tender creatures whose fur tickled his hands and whose teeth took the flesh from his bones.

During the day, however, there was a kind of order in the chaos. Order, that is, until Christmas Eve—the night Mrs Henry Gill came upon him beating the O'Dwyers' pet tabby, Constance, to death with a rolling pin.

Christmas Eve started at roughly 10 a.m., with several pots of decaffeinated coffee laced with brandy and sweets from the local French patisserie served from a hired silver tray. Henry Gill's office was alive with activity. After a couple of months in the political doldrums it was nearly Christmas, and—almost unbelievably—things were beginning to happen for the Party.

From the silver tray, Henry's sweet tooth forced him to pick the sugary cream-cakes. When midday came and the champers started popping he ate a couple more of the sweet cakes; his secretary, Marcella, had surreptitiously placed a few in his desk drawer for him, as she did every Christmas Eve and every Easter. As the others laughed and danced in the corridors Henry washed the cakes down with cold Moët et Chandon Brut, drunk out of a polystyrene cup. The polystyrene cups that the Party purchased, right across the country, were guaranteed to be made by a process which used no CFCs. The media had loved that story; it had been the Leader's own idea, bolstered, of course, by the advice of several aides and a White Paper on the subject. Within the Party and within the Government, everyone's dictionaries and thesauruses, whether paper or electronic, now readily fell open at the word 'environment'.

Donations to the Opposition had been good most of that year, then there had been the November/early December slackening-off period, but now, just at Christmas, when everyone was supposedly away and far removed from the woes of the economy and the environment, bumper donations! The Government *must* fall at the next election. True, it was more a case that the Government would lose rather than that the Opposition would win—a fine but important point—but, so what? Henry mused upon the implications as he swallowed the last of his cake and champagne. The Front Bench and Power. The all-potent position in Parliament, he alliterated with cream at the corner of his mouth. Power and Moët—he could feel his spirits rise.

At Luppino's, an Italian BYO they had been using for years, the office Christmas party started at 7 p.m. All were well and truly in a party mood long before then. Henry knew that it had been a hard year for everyone, but perhaps not such an unrewarding one after all. 'Power' was the unspoken word that was being bandied about more and more with every dead bottle of champagne that was thrown out Luppino's back door. Dancing on the restaurant tables didn't kick off until after Henry's speech, which was a powerful one, then the restaurant became a blur of dancing, drinking, eating, and more drinking.

Later, with a brimming cold glass of champagne, Henry Gill wandered off to the men's room. As he stood at the urinal he sipped from his glass, smiling to himself as his pee splashed his shoes. On his way back to the private dining rooms, Mary Durham, a new member of staff in administration, was having trouble negotiating the corridor in her high heels.

She cheered him when she saw him. 'Great speech!'

With a flourish Henry reached out and took her cold hand, bowing over it. Then, as they stood in the corridor, he on his way back from the men's, she on her way to the ladies', with the subtlety of a nightclub Casanova, Henry Gill pulled Mary Durham toward him. From her high heels she fell into his arms, and Henry kissed the thin, impressionable lips.

'Henry—'

He pulled Mary Durham further down the corridor, his lips not leaving hers.

'Henry,' she said again, when she could take a breath, then soon, because not-so-deep-down she had kind-of-always wondered about it with Henry Gill—the Boss—they were somehow already booked into the motel that Luppino's backed onto, a place which did a steady trade in this type of situation on these types of nights.

'What about the party?' she managed to say before all her clothes came off.

'The Party? I love the Party. I love the Party!'

Misunderstanding him, Mary Durham said, 'Yes—is it like this every year?'

'And every day!'

She unbuttoned Henry Gill's trousers, feeling around in the darkness because he had turned off the lights. What was this?

'Shorts—boxer shorts!' Mary laughed. Unable to see Henry's face, she delved more deeply. 'Oh come on now, Henry!' she said finally, looking up towards his grey face with disappointment.

Oh God—what had she said? He was the Boss! Vainly she tried to make everything all right—what were the words?

'It's all right, darling, I understand,' she said without much sincerity, but even as the words came out she felt herself pushed roughly aside, the hotel room door slamming loudly shut as Henry Gill fastened his buttons and escaped into the unwelcoming night.

It was just going on towards midnight, minutes to Christmas day, and Henry Gill was in his flannel pyjamas. A little too hot for summer, but it was a coolish night. Anyway, he had always liked the feel of flannel against his skin, ever since his childhood; it made him feel safe and warm and good. A good boy. Good.

Mrs Gill was asleep in the upstairs bedroom, her snores waiting to welcome Henry whenever he decided to call it a night. Her writers' group Christmas party had broken up quietly after 10 p.m., and Mrs Gill now slept the quiet slumber of a few too many soothing cups of unsweetened herbal tea.

There was a roaring in Henry Gill's ears: the kettle boiling, too much champers, Mary Durham laughing her 'Oh come on now, Henry' laugh as she delved too deeply.

And there was the incessant whining of the neighbourhood cats. For pity's sake—on Christmas Eve, no less! How could there be so many, how could people sleep with that damn racket, why hadn't the City Council done something about it? Henry felt the weight of his many questions and with trembling hands poured the boiling water. He saw Mary Durham's face in the instant coffee murk. He could picture that face of hers as she told the other girls the 'Oh come on now, Henry' story, and in their laughter at him they would all sound like—

Yowling cats!

Slamming the front door of his house open he stared wildly into the empty suburban streets, an angry middle-aged politician in flannel pyjamas. The legion of cats had hidden themselves in the gardens of the neighbouring homes. Cunning little neutered devils!

But there—there was one, *in flagrante* garden!

Wasn't that the fat fluffy neuter of the O'Dwyers? Socialists! What was the thing called?

'Puss,' he beckoned with a soft voice, 'puss-puss.'

The tabby darted up the front Gill garden and stopped, poised, illuminated by a street lamp and with its eyes shining blackly.

'Oh come on now, Puss,' he paraphrased Mary Durham.

Constance! That was the thing's name. And from where it sat watching between the Gill rose garden and the Gill garage, it wouldn't move. 'Constance,' he called in a hoarse whisper, but the dumb beast didn't know its own name. 'Wait there, wait there,' he said softly as he stepped quietly back into the kitchen. He rummaged around in the drawers and pantry, finally finding and opening a can of Nova Scotia smoked salmon.

Henry put the open can down on the doorstep in front of the door. In the fresh night the smell of canned salmon carried easily, and if Henry had been patient, within minutes a dozen cats would have found their way to his front step.

Still, he was gratified when the O'Dwyers' tabby came forward, nosing straight toward the can that now rested between his two feet. Constance quickly hunkered down between his slippers and the snuffling sounds made Henry's head spin.

Neutered, Henry thought as he lifted the rolling pin high. A nought, a nothing, a big fat zero. Asexual. Impotent and powerless. A vet with a thin face and a beak for a nose had cut away the furry testicles, Henry could see it happening in his mind's eye—even though Constance was female.

'Power,' he said, raising the rolling pin again.

From behind he heard, 'Henry!' but he didn't turn until the job was well and truly done.

Then he heard another name, 'Tommykins!', whispered, for even in times of great stress and great understanding Mrs Henry Gill had never been much of a screamer. Henry turned to her as she stood in flannel pyjamas that matched his. Even as he weighed the rolling pin in his hands he wished that he had checked to make sure the pantry was well-stocked with Mrs Gill's favourite tough green garbage bags.

It was daybreak on Christmas Day when Henry Gill awoke alone in his bed, sweating in his pyjamas, hands black with dirt. With his teeth he absently picked at the grit beneath his nails, listening to the high clamouring which had called him from sleep.

It was one, only one now. One insistent whine that was louder than any he had heard before, and he felt that the walls of the house should have been resonating with the cry. Were the neighbours up in arms? Where did it come from?

On bare dusty feet he wandered through the Gill home. Such a sound, such a terrible lament!

Henry went through the kitchen and out the front door. In the morning darkness he looked right around his detached garage and down the driveway, walked to the letter box at the front gate and checked up and down the street. No, not anywhere there. But then the whining came again and Henry Gill knew.

He picked his way around the neat brick home; mortgage figures jumped to his mind. He knew them backwards, knew the effect of each .05 per cent interest rate rise, knew almost from week to week what the magical lump sum payout figure was. This week it must be about—but he didn't go on. There were prickles in his lawn. Damn!

Henry walked onto the concrete path that followed the flower beds, then he was onto the grass again, morning dew cooling the bare dirty soles of his feet. He looked down at his hangnail, then remembered the dream of the cat gnawing his big toe. For a moment he felt a sense of fear, but the cry which came from under his beautiful brick house called him on.

He unlatched the plain wooden doorway that led into the cobwebs and dirt and misplaced tools under the Gill family home. As he entered that musty no man's land, the great tabby waited in between the many small freshly dug mounds of earth, its great teeth bared and ready to crush through the brittle bones of Henry Gill.

DOG

1 *Bella Pancia's Daughter*

Mario Faruggia had been back for three months, but if anything he felt stranger now than when his flight had first arrived. Luisa had been waiting in the little terminal for him, with her two cousins Paola and Veronica. What a shock those three had been! When he had left the small town of Piedemonte ten years earlier his daughter Luisa had been eight, the cousins ten and eleven apiece.

On his return from America, three women had been there to greet him. A Fiat Bambina, which Luisa had borrowed from her uncle, waited in the car park. She was the only one of the three girls to have a licence to drive. That made sense to Mario Faruggia: in a decade without a father a young girl had to learn independence, even in a place like Sicily.

So now, three months after that return, Mario walked into the streets of Piedemonte in the afternoon of a hot summer's day. He felt the strangeness of this place that used to be his home, the strangeness and the awkward familiarity.

The street was deserted, the square around the church and the police station abandoned, the doors of the three coffee shops closed and bolted. Mario thought of the ghost towns in the John Ford westerns he watched on television in Kate's apartment in lower Chicago, but here it was only the regular summer afternoon snoozing time. In a few hours everyone would be out again after a hearty lunch and a few hours in bed, Luisa included. But he was well and truly out of the habit and it was a point of issue with him not to relearn it. He was an American now, back in Sicily only to take his daughter Luisa away with him; if his wife hadn't died he could have stayed in lower Chicago and everything would have been easier.

Mario headed toward the empty town square. He really wished that he hadn't had to come back to Piedemonte. If his wife had just been more careful he could have stayed forever with Kate in her little apartment, he could have worked forever on the floor of O'Reilly's Ladies and Menswear Manufacturers—a good foreman, soon to be a good manager amongst the Irish executives. But one day the wife he had left behind in the small Sicilian town had reached too far for the soap powder on the top shelf of her little shop. La Signora Santiago had watched the legs of the little ladder tremble and tilt, but engrossed in her thoughts of how many shirts were in the dirty washing waiting at home, had done nothing to stop it.

And that had been that for Signora Faruggia.

Luisa had written to him and told him there was no need to come, but he had come anyway. Even with the space of so many years between them, he was still her father. And it was up to him to take her to something better, to a future—away from the little grocery shop on the Via Vecchio, away from Piedemonte, perhaps away from the whole country. There were places like America, after all.

But to his surprise, Luisa had her own ideas.

Mario Faruggia looked from the streets to the looming shape of the volcano, Mt Etna, *Etneo*—but he was out of the habit of thinking in Sicilian too. Kate, with that Irish smile and gentle manner, had kept him to the new language and he had been a good pupil. His mother tongue was now more or less foreign to him, but it was coming back—as were the memories of this place and these people who lived here. It was all against his will. He wanted to be back in lower Chicago with Kate in her little apartment, but he wanted too to get Luisa on a course out of Piedemonte.

He touched the small gold crucifix that hung on a chain around his neck. It was all his fault. He had left his wife and child behind as many men had to do in those days. At first it had been for a year, to get things organised. Then for another year because the money was bad. And then there had been O'Reilly's and the young machinist, Kate, and Sicily had seemed too far away.

From 1959 to 1969; Mario wandered alone and looked from Mt Etna to the clear sky. Tonight he and the relatives and friends and neighbours would sit on wicker chairs outside their homes and watch the moon. It was 18 July and Apollo 11 had been sent up two days earlier. No one in town believed that the Americans, or anyone else for that matter, were about to set men onto the moon. Luisa didn't believe it either. But they all watched the night sky anyway, in case of signs.

Tonight the interminable conversations would continue and Mario Faruggia would be obliged to listen to it all, for if he stayed indoors and refused to join the others in their wicker chairs and earthy-tasting bottles of wine, there would be talk. Ten years was a long time, but where Mario had forgotten the villagers of Piedemonte, they had not forgotten him. Or Signora Faruggia bringing up a little girl on her own, waiting so many years for the call from America. Mario joined them every night, unused to it all, to keep the peace and stop the talk about Faruggia bad blood.

Feeling that he had never been so alone in all his life, he wandered the bright, empty streets with the decayed stone homes of his relatives and neighbours tightly locked against the afternoon. He imagined the bars in Chicago, the drinks, the excitement of President John F. Kennedy's space travel promise coming true, and longed to be there. Here there was hardly even a television to see it when in a few days it might finally happen.

On a street corner facing Piedemonte's town square, a thin donkey stood alone in the sun, its head tied with bells, packs secured to its back and haunches. Its head was lowered. Mario wanted to untie the sad dumb beast and lead it to some shade, but the bells would tinkle and the owner would emerge from his sleep in a rage, believing that someone was trying to steal his donkey. He would see that it was Mario Faruggia and things might be worse.

Mario stood helplessly, his shirt sticking to his back. He lit an American cigarette and flicked the match onto the cobblestones. A dog was nosing its way around the hot square, cocking its leg against a broken statue of King Victor Emmanuel II then against the door of the town's police station.

The door of the police station opened and the chief of police, Ezzio Licastro, gently shooed the dog away. Mario raised his hand in greeting but Licastro looked through him, shutting the door once more.

The dog sat down, a dusty bundle, next to a bench and a wire litter bin. Mario remembered the little town square as it was during religious festivals, strung with coloured lights and coloured paper, music from three or four-piece bands playing, smoke in the air from the outdoor cooking of meat or chickpeas or bread. And Our Lady or some saint resplendent in white, up on an altar covered with wildflowers, with children in white clothes and white socks and white shoes on their knees before that altar, little hands pressed together as they mumbled their prayers through their white lace veils. Mario touched his gold crucifix hanging from its chain.

Luisa—how was he going to get her out of this place that was so frozen in the past?

With sadness he realised that even if it were 18 July 1999 the townspeople would probably still not believe that a country was sending men to the moon.

The dog twisted around and dug into its dusty haunches with its teeth. From that distance it was difficult for Mario to be sure but wasn't that Luisa's mutt with the worn-down teeth and fleas? Mario puffed on the heavy cigarette and squinted towards the square. What an insult—with age, not only was his girth still expanding, but his eyes were also getting weak.

Perhaps even in the silence of the sacred *mezzogiorno* he could afford a low whistle.

The dog pricked up its ears then rose to its thick strong legs. When Luisa had first brought her father home three months earlier there had been an afternoon's wariness from the dog, but that had been it. Now it was all Mario could do to keep the dog off him.

Luisa's dog shot like an arrow from the town square to the street. Mario grinned and whistled again, this time with a high pitch that made the sweltering donkey look up sharply. Mario squatted down and clapped his hands for the dog to come to him. In all of Piedemonte, Luisa's dog was the only thing that greeted him with enthusiasm.

A car coming around the corner—too fast!—the dog running into the street.

Mario saw two people in the front of the car, a man and woman, both with expressions of awful surprise. The skid of brakes, the slewing of tyres on cobblestones covered in donkey shit. Luisa's mutt! It reared sideways and would have been solidly hit if the driver hadn't jerked his steering wheel to the left. Too far—there was a crash and a crunch of glass. Mario's hand went to his crucifix as the dog bounded from the street, jumping straight into his arms, knocking him backwards.

'Great!' The driver was out of the car and around the other side, helping the woman out. In the sunlight she looked pale and harried. The car had rammed its right fender into a stone wall. A headlight was broken, the front windscreen had cracked but not shattered. With difficulty Mario picked himself up and stayed with the dog. He didn't want trouble and he could see that the two from the car were not Italian.

The driver was a young man in his late twenties or early thirties, the woman about the same age, but her pale face was severe and made her seem older. They were inspecting the damage, the man with his hands on his hips and sweat stains under the arms of his white shirt. The sleeves were rolled up but he wore a thin grey tie that he now tore from his collar and threw with anger into the car. He was looking around.

'Hey you—Luigi! You speak English? That your dog?' The woman took his arm as if to quieten him down but he jerked away. 'Does anyone around here speak English?' he said to the old stone walls and empty streets. 'Jesus, Heather, what luck!' He looked up at the distant volcano and pointed as if he had found the explanation. 'In the dark shadow of Vesuvius, what bloody luck!'

Mario was stroking the dog's head, hoping that one of the policemen from the station might appear, but there was no one. He longed to pull his old cap down over his eyes. He didn't want trouble, not here in Piedemonte. He wanted anonymity.

'You there—you know anyone around here that speaks English? That your dog?'

Mario would not meet the angry young man's eyes and continued to reassure Luisa's dog. It was trembling. Mario wanted to leave but he was afraid of the man coming after him; after all, the dog running across the street, the car swerving, the glass on the cobblestones, somehow it would all be made out to be his fault. The driver spat into the gutter in disgust and went back behind the wheel of the car. He started the engine and found reverse, but when the car moved there was an awful grinding.

'Great!'

The woman was looking up and down the street, her hands clutching a white handbag, her skirt cut to the knee and, Mario knew, too short for Piedemonte, Etneo.

'Look Henry, there's people coming.'

Mario looked too.

'I wonder if any of the natives can speak English—I wonder if they're even friendly. Get the phrase book and the glass beads. I think we're gonna need them.'

Mario knew that those who came out of their homes to look at the accident would come straight for him to help the foreigners; as far as he knew, the only other person in town who could get by with English was Dottore de Sica, and he would be getting ready to start his afternoon rounds. Mario fought the urge to pull his cap down over his eyes and take one of the side streets. Everything was against him, he thought hopelessly.

'Yes, mister,' he said softly as he walked across the street. 'I would like to help you.'

The man looked to his wife and back to the fat, dark Sicilian in old clothes and a moth-eaten cap.

'How much English do you speak?'

'Enough, signore, enough. I used to live in America,' he said, unable to stop himself speaking in the past tense. He went on unhappily, 'You are American?'

'No, we're not American. Listen, what do you do about things like this here? Can you arrange something for—' He waved at the car. A crowd was gathering and it wasn't lost on Mario Faruggia that no one seemed very pleased at having their afternoon sleep disturbed.

He could see them staring at him, could imagine them wondering: But that Faruggia, what trouble has he created now? Several voices called out to him asking what had happened.

'Crazy foreigners can't drive,' he said defensively, then stole a guilty glance at the two to see if they had understood.

'Well?' the man spoke, indicating the car again.

'You have rented the car? Perhaps you must telephone the company.'

'Huh, if only,' the other replied vaguely. 'It's mine, I own the damn thing. We've been on the continent six months. It was cheaper to buy a car and sell it later than to rent one—is there someone in town who can fix this thing?'

Mario walked to the side of the car that had driven into the wall. Others followed and studied the damage with him. It was only a cheap Fiat and the damage wasn't serious.

'I think you can drive it away without too much anxiety.'

'We can't take it away, we've already sold it,' the woman explained with a nervous smile. She held onto the strap of her handbag as if to a lifeline. 'To a man in Piedemonte, Etneo.' She took a piece of paper from her bag. 'A Signore Pasquale in the Via Tettranole. We were bringing the car to him.'

Mario Faruggia tried not to look as defeated as he felt. Everyone stared at him, the foreign couple included. Luisa's dog panted at his heel. Finally he turned to one of the younger boys in the crowd and spoke to him in Sicilian.

'Si, Bella Pancia!' the young boy said and he and three of his friends grinned and quickly ran off down the street.

'Please—' he said to the couple, and waved them toward the tables and chairs in front of one of the coffee shops near the town square. But the shop was shut. He looked desperately around the corner. The other two were shut in the *mezzogiorno* as well. All eyes remained on him. Mario felt the perspiration running down his forehead. He was defeated.

'Please—you will come to my home. The boys will fetch Signore Pasquale and he will come there. The boys will fetch the local mechanic and he will come to my home also. It may take some time, I am not certain. Please,' he continued quietly, wanting anything but this, 'we will have coffee or a cool drink if this pleases you. And your things, it is best to take them from the car.' He looked toward the sun. 'It is best to leave the car and go indoors.'

'Well that's good of you. This couldn't have come at a worse time. I can just see Mr Whatever-his-name-is pulling out of buying my car. That dog of yours—' He pointed to its head. Everyone's eyes seemed to swivel to Luisa's dog. 'But I appreciate your help, I really do—don't I, Heather?' Suddenly he put his hand to Mario, who looked at it as if he were about to be struck. 'My name's Gill, Henry Gill. And this is my wife Heather. What did that kid call you—Bella Punzer?'

'No, no, my name is Mario Faruggia.' He shook the younger man's hand quickly, his eyes looking down to the ground. He wasn't sure how much more humiliation he could bear in Piedemonte. 'Please, you will come to my home.'

He wanted the street to swallow him up.

There was a toothless grin here, a smirk there—this was something else about La Bella Sicilia that he was no longer used to. Since the age of about fifteen when he had first grown fat, people had called him 'Bella Pancia'—Beautiful Belly. In small towns there was a nickname for almost everyone. Even after ten years they don't forget, he thought with awe, quickly surveying the townspeople around him. And the little boy who had just called him by that name was no more than ten years of age!

Looking around at the old stone homes, at the old stone faces, Mario Faruggia despaired for Luisa.

'I've picked up a little of your language,' Henry Gill spoke as he pulled a small suitcase from the boot. Mario watched him— why wouldn't he leave the subject alone! 'I'm sure I heard something like "Bella Punzer". That's beautiful something—aren't I right? Beautiful something, something German, something military?'

'No, no, you are mistaken. Please—my home is this way.'

Mario Faruggia's face was gloomy as he led them down a side street redolent of fresh donkey shit.

In spite of the heat Henry and Heather Gill wanted a cup of tea.

In the little shop that was now Luisa's, Mario dug around the shelves for tea. He had no idea if there was any or not, but he tried to look confident.

'I'm surprised you stock it,' Henry Gill said. 'We've found it nearly impossible to get proper tea in Sicily. That's why we brought our own.'

The shop smelled of broad beans and chickpeas and oranges. All the fresh food came from local producers, the rest—Mario didn't have a clue. In a drawer he found two cartons of American baseball cards. His wife and Luisa must have wondered what to do with those!

Inside the shop it was much cooler than outside. The windows were shuttered and the front doors had been bolted. It was dark; Mario was despairing of finding tea. As if to mock him, three jars in a row that he opened held ground coffee.

'Really, it's all right. We do have our own. I was in your country in '63, and I learnt my lesson then. We've got some in the bag, haven't we, Heather? We'll have some good Australian tea, won't we, Mario?'

In the small living area, which was no more than a rough table and wicker chairs standing together, Henry and Heather sat down while Mario went to the wood stove. He put a bent old copper kettle over the main burner; it sat there as awkwardly as the two foreigners.

While Mario had his back to them, Henry pulled aside a curtain that seemed to divide the room. There was the main bed, made up beautifully with a lace spread and a perfect china doll sitting between the pillows. Henry winked at Heather and let the curtain fall.

The kitchen was a part of the same room. On Sundays they took a tin tub from the garden and pushed the table and chairs aside, and that was the bath. The room looked back to a square of garden where Luisa grew flowers and sweet potatoes and sometimes strawberries, and where rabbits, when they had them, stayed. It was the most pleasant part of the home. Henry and Heather stared out to it as Mario's wide, blunt fingers pulled back the folded edges of the Bushells' packet they had given him.

In the awkward quiet of the room Mario was nervous and spilled some of the tea onto the floor. Neither of the Gills moved. He wished that he could turn on the radio that stood by the sink, just for the noise. Mario glanced back at the two: Henry with his fists on his knees and Heather with her white handbag placed by her right foot, her hands lost and fidgety without the security of the bag's strap.

He wanted to say to the two of them:

—*But this is not my home, I live with Kate in a pretty apartment in Chicago, the United States of America. I left this place behind ten years ago. I read American newspapers and one day soon I will do adult courses in whatever takes my interest. I work for an Irishman, Mr Seamus O'Reilly. I am a foreman over twenty-three men and women, most of them Irish too, three of them Jews and one of them a young Greek girl. This is not my home and this man you see is not me.*

—And my daughter Luisa, just eighteen years of age. I will get her away from Piedemonte, Etneo. Like yourselves, one day she will be free to see the world and everything there is in it, she will see that there is more to life than she has known here in La Bella Sicilia. I will never let her marry a local boy with rough hands and the smell of onions and oil on his breath, to bring a new generation into this hopeless backwater ...

As the water boiled in the kettle—it didn't whistle for there hadn't been a whistle since before Mario had escaped to America—he called upstairs, 'Luisa, Luisa, we have guests.' He had forgotten that she spent the *mezzogiorno* in her own little room. The Faruggia family had always been a little more fortunate than others, there was the shop after all, and though there was only one room downstairs to be the main bedroom and sitting room and kitchen and bath, there was a small upstairs part that fifty years ago had been used for storing grain. There was a wooden shack in the garden too, that served as an outhouse. But most people had one of those, or at least a neighbour did.

By the time Mario Faruggia was serving the Australia tea into cracked clay cups, he could hear Luisa moving around upstairs. He thought of Kate's china teaset, the one they had saved months of their wages for, with its handpainted blue and yellow and red cups. Mario handed Henry and Heather Gill their tea as he prayed for the local mechanic and Signor Pasquale to come quickly.

But the thought stopped abruptly.

La Signora Gill was tasting the tea with a sour expression, but il signore was staring toward the roughly hewn stone steps that led to the small upper rooms. Luisa's dog lay in a grey heap at the foreigner's feet.

Mario followed Henry Gill's gaze.

She was coming down the steps rubbing her eyes. Bella Pancia's eighteen-year-old daughter.

He looked from his daughter to Henry Gill and back to his daughter again. The man had such a look on his face. That expression of surprise, that half-smile, and his wife right by him sourly tasting her Australian tea polluted with Sicilian water!

Mario sat down and stirred with a broken spoon in his broken cup. He didn't want to look at anyone.

'Please come and sit with us,' he said in Sicilian to his daughter. 'These people are stranded for a little while, try some of their tea.'

Finally he looked up to Henry Gill's preoccupied expression. But was it possible, at all possible?

Unconsciously, Mario Faruggia's free hand strayed to the gold crucifix that hung on its chain around his thick neck.

2 The Life and Loves of a Dusty Grey Dog

In the end Mario Faruggia had asked the Australians to stay in his home for the time it took for their car to be made ready. Signore Pasquale had come during the afternoon, and with a great sad face had indicated that once the repairs were done he would still be prepared to buy the Fiat. The grimy, greasy mechanic had picked his nose and mumbled, 'Cinque giorni, sei giorni', but Mario had been able to get him to promise three days for the job.

And when Bella Pancia had gone on to offer that they stay at his home for the time it took rather than trying to find a hotel in the nearest big town, Ranazzo, Henry Gill had been happy to accept. Even if the traveller's cheques had not been running low he would have accepted. The daughter had settled that. Heather Gill had taken up her handbag and had held the strap until her knuckles whitened.

That night there were many dusty bottles of wine. The two strangers sat on wicker chairs outside the small Faruggia store while the locals, people from the street and those nearby, yabbered at them, stared at them. Mario Faruggia had done the translating. Most of the conversation and questions were about the moon and Apollo II. To the peasants, Americans going to the moon was impossible; they weren't even able to comprehend that Australia and America were not one and the same place! Henry hadn't missed the embarrassment with which Faruggia had done the translations. Luisa and her two dumpy friends sat listening to the talk for a while and had grown bored, later wandering down the narrow streets for the evening's *passegiata*. Henry missed her when she went, had missed that straight black hair and dark eyes, the curve of her cheek. Had she smiled at him during the night a little longer than she needed to? He would have gone after them had there been the chance for him to slip away.

Later as he lay on the narrow mattress with his wife, Henry Gill laughed to himself at the embarrassed fat face of Mario Faruggia. Bella Pancia—Bella Punzer; Henry Gill liked that.

'That's beautiful something, aren't I right? Beautiful something, something German, something military?'

Fat Guts of course!

Italy had been interesting enough in Henry Gill's university days for him to do several semesters' worth of minor subjects in Italian, a balance for his political science majors. And he had done a quick round of Northern Italy back in 1963 before settling down with Heather. Of course he had picked up enough to understand a little peasant Sicilian.

They were upstairs in the room next to Luisa's. A small window set above head height let in a little air. Henry watched one lonely star twinkle out in the dark; otherwise it was totally black in the room. Never meant for people, Henry mused, but then Luisa's room would be no better.

With the thought of that girl in his mind he made love to

Heather. She was quiet because of Luisa next door; Henry Gill wanted his wife to cry out.

With the wine sour and warm in his belly, he lay falling asleep, but the sounds of Luisa quietly moving around in her room made his eyes open again. It was very late. He watched the single star, listening attentively, then he heard her door open and her soft footsteps as she went down the stairs. A glass of water, a visit to that disgusting shack in the garden? If only when she returned she would come into this room!

And he was on his feet and at his own door, standing behind it in the dark, waiting, listening. Heather was dreaming her tight little dreams and Mario Faruggia snored alone in the big bed downstairs. In a moment he heard the fall of Luisa's quiet footsteps as she returned.

Henry opened the door.

A light from somewhere—the moon those peasants believed was so inviolable?—shone on her hair, her profile.

Luisa stopped in mid-step just at the top of the staircase. She stared at him but her face showed nothing—what could she see of him? Henry wanted to go to her but his heart was beating too fast. She was holding a glass of water, her long hair was falling across her face. As they stared at each other, Luisa took a slow step back down one stair.

It was like a slap in the face to Henry.

He shut the door behind himself and returned to the hard mattress, to Heather stretched out in his absence. His heart would not stop racing.

Luisa was quickly back in her room. He heard something that sounded like a piece of furniture being moved and set down—a chair up against the door?

Henry Gill lay breathing hard, then he pressed his naked body to his wife and started waking her.

During the three months since his return to Piedemonte, Etneo, Mario Faruggia had been doing work here and there: help-

ing Massimo Pagano with the new tiles for his roof, building a
stone wall to keep the chickens and the rain out of the widow
de Tullio's little patch of garden, some work with Giovanni from
next door.

Giovanni was an old man now, thin and with a tubercular
cough and sunken dry cheeks, but he still owned a small vineyard on the fertile land around Mt Etna. Mario had been going
with him every morning for a week now, their long walk there
starting at 5.30 a.m. Even with his foreign guests sleeping in the
home, Mario waited at his doorstep for Giovanni, who would
soon arrive smoking a worn-down old butt and leading his
donkey.

An old jumper he hadn't worn in over ten years but had
found in a drawer beside the bed kept the morning cold away.
He stared at Mt Etna as he waited. The name of the town—Piedemonte—meant 'foot of the mountain', and he remembered
his father's stories of the eruptions and the lava. Even now in
the morning mist before the sun was properly out, he could see
the red glow coming from the yawning mouth of the volcano.
When he had been a child it had seemed so natural, now it was
like a persistent bad omen.

Too much wine with the foreigners; he rubbed his cheeks
and stamped his feet. Nearly two hours to the vineyard and two
hours back; this morning he wasn't looking forward to any of
it, and Luisa was on his mind as well. The tinkling bells of the
donkey could be heard from next door. Giovanni would be ty-
ing his packs to the beast's flanks.

One of the first things Mario had done when he came back
from America and met Giovanni again had been to resole the
old man's boots for him. They had been lined with newspaper,
perhaps for a whole year.

As Mario watched the red heart of the volcano and wondered about Luisa and the foreigners, the old man and beast
came slowly around the corner, bells tinkling. One day when
Giovanni's luck ran out Mario would bring him home strapped

to the donkey's back like a sack of potatoes. They were too old here in Piedemonte, or too young. Soon they would all be gone, Luisa too.

Smoke from Giovanni's cigarette drifted off into the morning. He wore an old cap that was the same as Mario's, pulled down over the small watery eyes, and Mario pulled his down too as he walked toward the donkey.

'It must happen soon,' she said.

Henry leaned back in the hard seat and drew on his cigarette. It was the morning of 19 June. A man slowly drinking a cup of coffee across from them was engrossed in an Italian newspaper. Henry stared at what headlines he could see: 'Luna', 'NASA', and—strangely—'Hollywood'.

'Of course it must,' he replied, but the distant Mt Etna was dry and stony, and so was the sky.

'Six months,' Heather continued, looking at the last of her coffee.

'And how long have you been off?'

'You know how long. Since my birthday.'

'And still—' He left some greasy notes on the white saucer. The coffee had tasted somehow stale; too weak to be bitter, too strong to be bland. 'Come on, Heather,' he said, putting out his cigarette in the coffee cup and taking her hand. 'It's a beautiful day.' It struck him that his words were as stale as the coffee. He looked at his wife's pale face then back to the barren hills which led to the mouth of the volcano. 'Let's walk.'

He kissed her quickly and as he drew away he noticed the lines at the corners of her mouth, the blueprint for the coming years. Of course she was right, if they were going to start it must be now. She wanted four; there had been twins in her family for generations. Was it true that they always skipped a generation?

But he was glad there was nothing yet, no signs, no plans that had to be made. But if it did not happen soon there would have to be tests to determine whether they really could or not. Henry felt a dual sense of frustration. Frustration that six months had passed with nothing happening, frustration that finally soon he would be committed. Forget wedding vows. Heather no longer taking her pills—that was commitment.

As they walked in the sunshine Henry put his arm around Heather's shoulders and Luisa's dog tagged after them. Heather turned her white face to him. In the real estate office he had franchised back home there had been Anna Wheeler, the lady handling prestige properties. At the local Party meetings there was Edna Goodfellow. Here in Italy, six months of looking at beautiful Mediterranean girls—then, finally, Bella Pancia's daughter, Luisa.

Her dog, grey and dusty and stocky, urinated against a gutter. Heather made a small annoyed sound. The way she dragged her feet on such a warm and bright day annoyed him.

'Didn't you sleep well, darling?'

In the morning they had been sitting at one of the open terraces near the town square facing the police station. Several of the old men had nodded at them; their first coffees had come courtesy of the owner, who had drunk much of Mario Faruggia's wine the night before while listening to the *Americani* explain that NASA and Hollywood were not one and the same thing. But that morning, without Mario to translate, no one had been able to speak to them. A stocky girl with terrible acne had at one stage breezed past their table and said, 'Good morning, my two friends,' but when Heather had replied to her it was obvious the girl could not understand a word. Ezzio Licastro, the chief of police, had also gone by, stiffly saluting them with 'Complimenti, complimenti,' and continuing on to the station though Henry had waved him over.

Forgetting what they had originally been talking about, Henry now said, 'It must be soon now,' and felt in his pockets for change so that he could buy a newspaper from the tobacconist's they were passing.

'You mean the landing?' Heather said quietly.

As Henry studied the small coins in his hand, Luisa's dog cocked its leg against the tobacconist's door. He pushed the dog aside and went into the shop, emerging with the daily newspaper from Palermo.

'What does it say?' Heather asked, and the dog looked up at him too. Heather took a handkerchief from her handbag. 'It's so hot.'

'I don't know what it says. "Armstrong, Aldrin, Collins",' he read. 'Something about an uninviting surface, some dates. "LM", "CM", nothing much else that I can translate. I'll save this paper for Faruggia, but I'm not sure he can read, of course. They land on 20 July—tomorrow!—around one or two in the afternoon, EDT. I wish there were papers in English to buy. Bit wasted here, I suppose.'

'LM—Lunar Module,' Heather spoke with the white lace handkerchief pressed to her forehead. 'Or Landing Module.'

'Very good, darling!'

'CM—Command Module.'

They walked on and the dog followed.

Beside the shade of an olive tree in front of the sandy playground of a school, Heather asked if they could sit down.

'I wonder how many kids there are in that school? Have you noticed there are never any young people in these bloody towns? People our age, I mean. The kids, when they grow up, they must just bugger off for the bigger cities. Imagine growing up in a place like Piedemonte and getting stuck here. Wouldn't you want to get out as soon as you could!'

Heather leaned back in the bench. 'Now you're getting the picture, Henry.' She wiped her lips. 'Can't we go somewhere else, for heaven's sake? I mean, it's not very interesting in Piedemonte—'

But Henry ignored her. 'Faruggia told me last night that his daughter is very lonely. Not many young men around. And she's only eighteen. And her mother died three months ago.'

'She's a beautiful girl.'

'D'you think so?' His manner was breezy and indifferent. 'I guess in a peasant sort of way. Like a good donkey or a mule.' He laughed for a moment at his own joke, then indicated the volcano. 'Wonder what it's like when that thing blows.'

Heather didn't answer. Henry leaned down and scratched the dog's ear but was watching the side of his wife's face. There was a lump along the ridge of her nose that she swore she would one day have removed by surgery. And the wrinkles? Or would the world finally be perfect when the babies were on the way?

'I like it here,' he said, as if she had complained again. 'And we need to wait for the car to be fixed. Where would we go anyway?'

'Where? Dear me. There's Taormina for a start. Then there's Agrigento, Salerno, or any of the main cities—Catania, Palermo, Messina. What about the coast and the beaches? What about the mountains? Dear, there's a hundred pages in the guidebook about La Bella Sicilia!'

'Still—' He continued scratching the dog's dirty ear. 'We need the money from the car.'

The dog rose quickly, its nose in the air. Henry watched the muscled forelegs twitching.

There was another dog, a bitch, and in the midday heat they started together right in the small children's playground. Henry Gill thought: the good southern dirt and the hot sun, earthy red wine, the town at the foot of Mt Etna. He thought of Luisa on the top step, staring at him, the dark hair across her face.

Heather's eyes were closed and she would not watch the dogs; Henry observed them closely. In the heat his shirt clung to his back.

Somewhere down one of the cobbled streets a radio played an Italian version of Tom Jones' recent hit, 'Delilah'.

It was in the *mezzogiorno* that the two foreigners came back. Luisa had shuttered the windows and closed the doors, but she hadn't locked them, knowing that the two would have to return sometime. By now Luisa should have been upstairs in her room, dozing on the hard bed in her slip, but the foreigners had broken her routine. She swept the floors and dusted the shelves just to keep occupied, and she made a pile of rubbish on the floor. When she heard the two coming through the front door she rushed into the back and busied herself at the stove.

It had been difficult to sleep during the night. All the talking outside, the two foreigners making love in their room, the man standing in the doorway at the top of the stairs in the middle of the night. Luisa had only stared at his face—she had no idea that he had been standing there naked.

They came through the shop and Luisa continued stirring in the small saucepan. She was making them chickpeas and pasta for lunch, but she hoped that they wouldn't want any and would simply go up to their room. Nervously, she put her hair back and stirred.

The woman's skin was bad and she seemed tired. The man, Henry Gill, smiled at Luisa.

'Buongiorno, signorina,' he said with the half-smile that never seemed to leave his face when he looked at her.

'Buongiorno.' She was about to say something about lunch but didn't know how to communicate it. She found it easier to go back to the saucepan and keep stirring.

But they did go on up the stairs!

Luisa breathed a heavy sigh of relief. Maybe by the time they were finished their afternoon nap her father would be back from Giovanni's vineyard and things would be easier for her. She would escape until the evening, might even stay at Santina's or Maria's for the night. She was used to peace in her house—since her mother had died, first her strange American father, now the two visitors. It was just too much!

Luisa spooned out a small bowl of the lunch for herself. She wasn't really hungry but she didn't want to waste it. The rest she would save for her father's dinner. And theirs, if that was what they wanted. The taste of the chickpeas made her feel better, but then there was the sound of the door upstairs opening, someone coming down the tight stairs.

He smiled at her, nodded at the saucepan, Henry Gill on his own and wanting lunch. He was saying something but Luisa could not understand a word. Bits and pieces might have even been her own language, but she was too nervous to listen properly—anyway, that strange accent of his distorted every word.

She rose from the small table and went to the stove, ladling him out a large serving. She also cut him a thick piece of fresh sour bread. Henry Gill walked to the stove and stood close to her; for a moment she could almost have believed that he was going to touch her.

Instead, his hand went to the old radio that stood by the sink. He turned it on and the sound was too loud, but he didn't seem to care. Luisa flashed him a look and turned it down herself. He was smiling at her again—why wouldn't he just go back up to his wife?

He was still saying something as she handed him the bowl. What else did he want? Was he really saying something in Italian? That accent!

'Cosa, signore?' she said out of politeness. Luisa sat down and faced, not Henry Gill but her own bowl of chickpeas and pasta. But then she did look up to him. In his white shirt and thin tie he looked like an American actor. She couldn't remember which one, maybe Montgomery Clift. She imagined him in America—she had no concept of a country called Australia—in the American big house where he lived, in the American big glass building where he worked and made a fortune over and over again.

He was repeating two words very slowly.

'Cosa—?'

Finally, 'Ti piace?'

She understood. He was asking her if she liked something. What—the house, the lunch, him? He pointed toward the radio.

Ah, the music. She listened to it politely, some heartbroken love song imported from another country.

'Non mi piace,' she said with a shake of her head, and shrugged.

He was indicating that he didn't like it either, then he said, 'Cosa?' with a shrug of his own shoulders. He wanted to know what music she did like. Her hands were tense at the effort it took to understand him. Luisa tried to think of some music he might know—the Beatles, beautiful Paul McCartney?—but it seemed impossible for her to pronounce the names. Why wouldn't his wife call out for him from upstairs?

Finally, she said, 'Kinx.'

He stared at her. 'What the hell is that?' he asked in English. She stopped herself from sighing and said it again, 'Kinx.'

'Ah!' Henry Gill's hands held his bowl tightly as he sat down next to her, pulled his chair close to her. His face was shining as he leaned toward Luisa. 'Si, si, Kinks. The Kinks.'

She nodded—this was boring her, but he started in a low soft voice:

'The only time I feel all right
Is by your side
Girl, I want to be with you
All of the day
All day, and all of the night
All day, and all of the night.'

Luisa stared at his nervously smiling face. It sounded terrible, and that accent. Was he serious? She didn't know whether to laugh or just hold herself as steady as she could. She knew the song, but he was so absurd! Luisa couldn't help herself.

But it was all right—he was laughing too. And how happy he seemed. Then he was asking her what else. She was going to say 'Engelbert Humperdinck' but that would have been as obvious as saying 'Tom Jones'. She thought of the dances in Zaffarana she went to once a month with her two girlfriends. What did the boys talk about?

She pursed her lips to try to get it right. 'Oo.'

His face was a blank.

'Oo,' she persisted.

Suddenly it registered. Henry Gill licked his lips and grinned.

'I can see for miles and miles
I can see for miles and miles
I can see for miles and miles and miles
And miles
Oh yeah.'

Luisa clapped her hands and couldn't stop laughing. She tried to keep as quiet as she could, it wasn't right to be making such a noise in the middle of the day with everyone sleeping— especially not with the American, Henry Gill.

But he was trying to be so nice and he was so funny. The more she laughed, she could see, the happier he was. And she had resented him and his wife so much! He was a nice man after all, and a very funny man. She imagined the great cities Henry Gill lived in, and pictured Tullio, the local mechanic, who called on her every Saturday night and who had picked his nose as he mumbled to the foreigners, 'Cinque giorni, sei giorni'.

She was too shy to look at Henry Gill so when she said, 'Can-te bello', the first words she had volunteered to him, it was to her bowl of cold chickpeas.

His eyes narrowed as he tried to understand, but in the dimness of the Faruggia kitchen while the rest of Piedemon-te—Heather included—slept, it was easier to lean closer to Luisa. She looked at him. For a moment he might have been listening for any sounds from upstairs. Luisa took up her spoon and looked back to the bowl. Henry Gill quickly kissed her lips.

Luisa pushed her chair back; Henry Gill did the same. Her bowl clattered into the sink as she went here, there. There was a loud crash—Henry has thrown his bowl into the sink as well, but his had broken. He looked defiantly at her, then that smile, that smile. He was talking again and she couldn't understand a word, she wouldn't listen. But he closed in on her and she was pressed to a wall; Luisa could smell his mild aftershave. Where was his wife, where was her father? In a moment she would cry out.

Henry Gill didn't press to her, but he would not let her go. His smile tried to make everything all right—one finger went to his lips and his eyes glanced upward. He was telling her to keep quiet for his wife!

It was easier to let him put his lips to her cheek, then to her neck, but when he kissed her lips again she managed to push past him. Down through the store, the doors banging shut behind her, out into the sunshine of the empty street. She breathed deeply, but he was behind her. Luisa looked up and down the Via Vecchio. What could she do—run down the street like a mad woman?

She had to get away. Going inside again she picked up as much as she could from the pile of rubbish. When Henry Gill followed her she made him pick up an armful too. Make him work! She could have thrown everything into his face, she was so angry, but this was better. When something fell from her own arms he bent, like a gentleman in an American movie, and took it up himself.

Out in the street once more, Luisa decided not to worry about the *mezzogiorno*. Let her neighbours talk! She would not go back inside with him. He was grinning all the while, as if he had everything in the world to be happy about. The grey dusty dog followed as they carried their loads of garbage down the Via Vecchio.

Henry didn't know where they were going and he didn't care. He wasn't quite sure how he had ended up with an armful of garbage. The street might have been hot and the perspiration might have been running down the side of his face, but all he could feel was the taste of Luisa's skin. She was tall, her long black hair fell to her shoulders, there was not a sign of make-up. Peaches and cream complexion, and on a diet of pasta and chickpeas and sweet potatoes from the back garden!

Without looking at him once, Luisa led him down the sloping streets to the outskirts of Piedemonte. He could not have found his way back if he had tried. There was the beginning of a clear stream, a broken stone bridge that carried what traffic there was through the town, and a thrown-together shanty town of rags and drab tents and woodfire smoke. Near the bridge's wider reaches, a group of gypsies slept and kept chickens.

The town's garbage dump was under and around the bridge. Henry and Luisa and the dog walked along the stream's wide flat rocks to get there. A few children were playing further down with their feet splashing in the shallow water and their cries echoing under the bridge. Some gypsies in rags that might once have been colourful started another fire across the stream from them and the smoke billowed up into the hot summer's day. Luisa went straight to the yawning mouth of the bridge and tossed her rubbish into the semi-dark. The children's echoes sounded out from the stony underbelly then the roaring of a truck passing above drowned them out.

The stone and concrete supports trembled under the truck's weight. Henry did as Luisa had done—down in the dark where running feet made the water splash, he thought he saw a dozen young children playing amidst the rotten, crowded garbage. The smell made him want to be sick and he went quickly back to Luisa, his collar damp with sweat and his shirt filthy.

Across the stream, Henry saw the start of the forests that grew around the lower reaches of the great volcano. It was all so fertile and rich and green. He saw abundant pine, chestnut and beech trees. That was where Henry wanted to be with Luisa, not standing on these white flat stones with the rubbish smell in the air.

'It looks fantastic over there, Luisa.'

All she recognised was her name. Luisa was throwing stones for her dog and Henry wondered if she had forgiven him. She saw where he was looking and she pointed up to the trees.

'Il regione boscosa,' she said. In spite of what he had done, or maybe because of it, Luisa wanted to tell him everything she knew about Mt Etna. Now that they were away from her home and out in the open there was no more threat from Henry Gill. This was her place and she knew everything about it. He could keep his American cities and piles of money.

Even though he couldn't understand, she said, 'Il regione coltivata, e poi il regione boscosa, e poi il regione deserta.'

Henry was looking at her, unaware of what she described. There were three regions to Mt Etna, each distinct and with its own characteristics. At the base was the fertile land where the farmers' produce came from and which was cultivated all year round; then there was the forest belt that Henry had been staring toward; finally there came the desert regions, where the ground was dead and the hills were all lava flows and caves and volcanic ash.

Luisa stood still for a moment. Could he understand that this was her place, that this was where she was meant to stay in spite of all the arguments her father had up his sleeve? She bent for another stone and threw it for her dog.

Henry walked to her and took her hand. He stood close and tried awkwardly to kiss her. In front of the gypsies.

America!

Luisa pulled away, but when he tried to kiss her again she suddenly swung hard and cracked him across the face with her open hand. The sound was so loud that the gypsies across the stream stared for a moment, then went back to their smoky fire.

With stars in his head and his hand at the right side of his face, Henry went quietly along the side of the stream. Jesus! Nothing like that had ever happened to him before.

When Luisa turned away he started to watch her again. She went off in the opposite direction, picking up stones and throwing them for the dog. The dog ran to the dust the stones raised and that was all.

'Great game,' Henry said to no one.

He picked up some flat stones himself and splashed them into the stream. He tried skimming them but even as a child he had never had the knack. His arm was uncoordinated. Even Heather could make three skips. The side of his face hurt.

A fat white chicken picked its way by him. Damn Luisa!

He threw his last stone hard at the chicken and there was a *thomp* and a sharp squawk as the chicken dashed dustily away. Henry saw another and took up a stone, throwing it hard but only raising dust in front of the sharp beak. The chicken was staring stupidly at where the stone had hit the dust. Henry tried again and hit it in the side. It squawked loudly and with feathers flying started running, which made the few others scatter. Henry bent for more stones.

Luisa was rushing toward him. She couldn't believe what he was doing. The gypsies too, half-sitting, half-standing, looked on in disbelief at the madman in the white shirt.

Luisa tried to knock the stones from his hands. Henry pulled his hands back then danced away. The dog barked and jumped between them. Luisa lunged for his hands again and Henry laughed, twisting out of her reach. Tears of frustration came up in Luisa's eyes. The American *was* mad! Her dog barked and jumped, barked and jumped.

But suddenly, laughing so that everyone could hear, Henry Gill threw all his stones high, straight up into the air so that they rained down like hail over them.

'Catch me, Luisa—bet you can't!'

He teased her and taunted her, but the tears in her eyes went away when he loudly sang,

'I can see for miles and miles
I can see for miles and miles

I can see for miles and miles and miles and miles
And miles ...'

She ran after him, caught a shred of his shirt-tail, nearly
had his hair.

'Try harder, Luisa, try harder!'

In his socks and shoes he crossed the stream, the water halfway to his knees, the afternoon hot and stark and dry. Luisa
gripped her skirt in both fists and cried out.

With awe, the small group of tired, dirty gypsies watched
as the tall girl with the black hair and flowing skirt chased the
madman into the quiet shade of the forest, the barking of the
dog leading their way through the thick trees.

3 The First Men in the Moon

'When I was a young man in Piedemonte, there were terrible
eruptions, 1950, 1951. Two towns near here, Ranazzo and For-
nazzo, nearly finished.' Mario Faruggia dusted off his hands.
'Tutto completo—nearly all gone. Everybody was evacuated
but not one person hurt. And when they came back, the lava
somehow had gone right around both towns. Is true, signora, is
a very famous case.' He nodded then smiled. 'Many prayers al
nostro Padre, si? Al Signore, you know, Mrs Gill?'

They sat together watching the morning sunshine, the wicker chairs placed in the shade just beside the shop's front step.
Luisa was inside scooping grain out of a barrel and weighing it
for Signore and Signora Lorenzo, two of the worst bad debts in
town. Yet everyone was, one way or another.

Henry Gill was just now returning from seeing the mechanic
about their Fiat. Heather could see him at the top of the Via
Vecchio, a long way off in the morning heat, a tall figure in a
white shirt coming down toward them.

'But in 1852 it was much worse, Mrs Gill. Everyone remember. It was more than one hundred years ago but no family can

forget something like that. Near Zaffarana, hundreds of people were trapped and died. There was no way to help them.' Mario stroked his moustache, it was a long time since he had remembered these things. 'And in the 1920s, one whole town called Mascali, swallowed up completely.'

They looked toward Mt Etna and Mario was amused by Heather Gill's expression.

He didn't know that she had only been half listening to him. There were other things on her mind, much more important matters. She watched her husband coming down the street, the heat shimmering above the cobblestones.

'Mr Faruggia,' she started quietly. 'My husband loves Sicily so much, did you know that? And I'm afraid I've been a wet blanket for him all along, especially in the last few weeks. All these months of travelling have taken their toll on me, and it hasn't been easy for Henry to get the most out of'—she looked around and smiled, spreading her hands—'all this.'

Mario Faruggia slowly turned his face to her. Was she making fun of him?

'What I mean to say, Mr Faruggia, is that I think he would dearly love to see more of the area.' She glanced up toward the great volcano again. 'That is a sight indeed. The guidebook says there are many interesting walks up the hills, and we do have time to spare. Or maybe the vineyards where you've been working. Things like that are unknown where we come from. But me, I'm just tired out ...' She smiled at him again.

He nodded slowly. 'Yes, Mrs Gill, I understand.' The dregs of coffee in his cracked little cup caught his eye. Luisa's dog lay in the shade a little way from them. Mario was already thinking ahead. Since the arrival of the Gills he could not get his thoughts of Luisa out of his mind.

'My husband wouldn't ask you, he wouldn't want to put you out, but I know that he would dearly love to see the countryside. I know this is your day off.' Heather spoke quickly now, Henry was nearly there. 'But could you take him around today, show him something of the—'

Henry walked from the sunshine into the shade where they were sitting. He looked hot.

'What does "tre giorni" mean in Sicily—a month?' He put his hands on his hips and looked around the squat stone houses. 'Jesus Christ, it's hot. That good-for-nothing has hardly touched the car. I can just see Pasquale pulling out of the whole deal.' Without seeming to, Henry tried to look into the shop for Luisa. 'Mario, why don't you speak to that lout again?'

Mario Faruggia was fiddling with the old pocket watch Kate had given him for his forty-third birthday. He remembered the pawn shop she had purchased it from, he remembered how happy she had been to give it to him, wrapped in pink crepe paper and with a card.

'Mr Gill, I spoke to him for you last night.' He made a quietening gesture with his hand. 'He assured me that by tomorrow evening—'

'Well, it'll be a miracle.'

Mario smiled—but this was the country of miracles. His gold crucifix shone in the sunlight. 'I also spoke to Signore Pasquale. He wants your car, it is a good price.'

'Have to sell it.' He wanted to look into the shop but the sunlight was shining off the glass so that he could see nothing. 'Holiday's just about done. Except for a month's cruise home on the *Achille Lauro*.' Suddenly he laughed, desperately. 'What do you think of that, a whole flipping month, Mario!'

The other nodded but said nothing. When the time came that he could finally return to Kate, he didn't want the journey to take a month. Mario looked at Mrs Gill, sitting quietly on the chair, her face tight and pale. If things went well, she would be the victim. Everyone else would be happy—even Luisa, one day. For a moment he couldn't look either of them in the face so he stared again at the face of his watch.

He searched for the right words, he wanted to get everything right.

'Mr Gill, it is very early.' The words should have been simple. It wasn't early at all, but he went on, 'I must go to Giovanni's vineyard today. Not a great deal of work, just some little things I did not finish yesterday.' Some little things? His sense of shame was beginning to overwhelm him. 'Perhaps you would like to come with me—la signora tells me that you have had little chance to see—' He glanced at Mrs Gill and back to his pocket watch.

'It's bloody hot today. Thanks anyway.'

'You should go with Mr Faruggia, Henry.'

'It's a day for staying in the shade with a cool drink,' Henry told her. He could just make out some movement in the shop. 'I know you're not feeling well, I should be with you.'

'It is very beautiful,' Mario said, but he stopped himself from going on. Henry Gill's manner was so distant it was like trying to interest a blind man in a sunset. 'We were hoping ...'

Henry Gill ran a hand through his short hair. 'We?'

Mario shrugged. 'Luisa and I.'

Henry put his hands in his pockets, turned around to the bright street. 'So you're closing the shop, then.'

'Today Luisa only keeps it open for a few hours in the morning.' Mario looked down at the broken knots of his bootstraps. It was hopeless. She was his problem. In the country of miracles, these kinds of miracles never occurred.

The two customers were leaving the shop and the bell above the doors tinkled with their departure. They nodded toward the two foreigners but said nothing to Mario.

'But what do you want, darling?'

Heather smiled. 'Henry, please go with Mr Faruggia. A day of quiet is just what I need. I've got that Jacqueline Susann to finish and you'll be back in the afternoon, I presume. Maybe by then I'll have surprised you all.' Her skin seemed translucent, her eyes misty. 'There might be one of my special dinners waiting for you and Mr Faruggia and the girl.'

'Well—' Henry wavered and hoped it looked sincere. 'I guess that sounds interesting. When will we get started, Mario?'

Henry Gill went indoors. Luisa was counting a pile of coins on the counter—for once the Lorenzos had paid straight away. She looked up at him and he put a finger to his lips, then quickly waved for her to follow him into the back.

Luisa's cheeks were red. Against the tiny stove they held each other and kissed. Anyone could have come in on them. When they separated Luisa stared at him, then took his face in her hands.

But Heather and Faruggia were coming into the shop. Henry went quickly into the small garden and fumbled with the latch of the rotting outhouse. His face was hot. By the time he had scooped sand into the filthy tin and returned, Heather had already gone upstairs.

Mario Faruggia had his back turned; with excitement Luisa made a hill of her forearm and with two fingers showed Henry a figure walking up it.

He took the steps two at a time to say goodbye to his wife. It was 20 June 1969.

He was surprised at how out of breath Henry Gill was, after all, the foreigner was the younger man. They had walked through the fields and along the river banks, then up through the hills that were once owned by the padrones of long ago.

Luisa was at the crest of a long rise; to her left would be cornfields, to her right—Mario Faruggia tried to picture it, but he couldn't remember exactly. It was only when he caught up with her that he saw the groves of olive trees and orange trees, fields of vegetables. The land looked rich and abundant.

'No one makes any money from the land,' Mario said when Henry Gill had also reached the crest.

But Henry wasn't interested. His breathing came hard and his face was covered in sweat. He was wearing a clean flannel shirt and it was soaked almost right through. He looked at Luisa. She was pulling at a straight branch to make herself a walking stick.

Mario followed Henry's gaze and smiled. She was as healthy and strong as he had been when he was eighteen—these hills back then, nothing to climb.

What never changed was the poverty, the hands in the dirt. And poverty followed him. In lower Chicago, the rent of Kate's apartment alone took most of their wages.

As he caught his breath, Mario Faruggia stared across the fields, across the mountains, over Mt Etna. In ancient Greek mythology, people had believed that the volcano kept the sky from falling down. Under Etna there slept a giant named Typhon, and whenever he twisted and turned the countryside trembled and the mountain spewed fire. He and Kate had spent a weekend at the local library looking up things like that. Now the mythologies were all gone—except that later today the first men to walk on the moon would be televised around the world, and no one in Piedemonte would believe any of it.

The three of them started walking again, Luisa in the lead using her straight branch like a band-leader's baton. In her peasant dress and strong straight stride, Mario knew that she belonged to these hills. He belonged too, with his 'bella pancia' and dark eyes and thick dark moustache, but that didn't change the fact that in another country an Irish girl called Kate waited for his return.

And as with him, anything anywhere in the world could have been waiting for Luisa. If only he could convince her.

Luisa ran down the last slope to Giovanni's vineyard. She knew all the vineyards of that particular hill for they were all worked by men and women from Piedemonte. The hill was called Bazzio, and she had been going there since she was a little girl. The shop had really made nothing for her and her mother, so work had to be taken whenever it was offered, even if the wages were no more than a lunch of olives and cheese, or an evening's plate of lentils and boiled carrots.

It didn't matter to Luisa. The hills were what she knew and

the people were what she knew; if she wanted cities, there was Zaffarana for the dances, Riposto for the beaches, Catania for the shops. She didn't need anything else. And always there was the Via Vecchio, her shop and her narrow bed, and the vineyards around Mt Etna.

But now too there was the American, Henry Gill. As she ran she looked back but he was far, far behind. Luisa used her scarf to tie her hair into a ponytail.

There were no fences to separate one vineyard from the next, but Giovanni had an old locked shed on the rise overlooking the descending narrow terraces and layers of his vineyard. Luisa knew under which rock the key was hidden. She quickly found it and unlocked the old brittle door. Inside it smelt of dirt and clay and old hay. Once during a terrible storm when none of them could get back to Piedemonte from Bazzio, she and her mother and Giovanni and the donkey had all slept together on the floor of the shed, the donkey moaning throughout the night because of the rolling thunder.

Luisa found a large ceramic water pot and took three clay bowls from a pile, placing them on the rich grass in front of the shed. Black ants hurried across a mound of dirt. She carried the heavy water pot down the hillside, skipping down from terrace to terrace until finally she was at the bottom, where Giovanni was lucky enough to have inherited a well.

Luisa filled the pot with cold underground mountain water then carried it back up the hill. Halfway up, at the terrace that she knew gave the best grapes, she put the heavy pot down and filled the front of her skirt with bunches of green grapes straight from the vine. She checked that there was no one to see, for in carrying the grapes in the front of her dress, her legs were exposed. Luisa hefted the water pot onto one shoulder, her other hand gripping the threadbare edge of her skirt. Like her mother and grandmother before her, she took each terrace as easily as if she carried nothing.

In front of Giovanni's shed she poured water into the clay

bowls and set out bunches of grapes onto the grass beside each one. They still hadn't arrived. A black ant scurried across the grapes meant for Henry; she squeezed it hard between thumb and forefinger.

Luisa took a deep breath and let it out with a sigh. The green and brown Sicilian fields were before her. As she looked out across the hills around them, a scent of wildflowers was carried up to her on the fresh mountain breeze.

Henry Gill felt sick with exertion. He had a stomach cramp and he longed to move his bowels, but when finally they arrived and he fell down onto his backside, the cold water and grapes made him feel better.

Luisa was smiling at him. When she did, it was as if Heather was a million miles away and Bella Pancia just didn't matter at all. Faruggia was talking and Henry Gill didn't want to listen. What homey Sicilian garbage would he be on about now?

'Down these hills, in the last war, my father saw an American fighter plane crash and explode. The pilot had tried to parachute but—'

They sat there, the three of them, facing the rolling countryside, Giovanni's fertile vineyard descending below. Luisa, Henry, Mario Faruggia. Luisa was edging her hand across the grass toward Henry's, he moved his toward hers, and as the old man continued talking they sat with a space of a few inches between the tips of each other's fingers.

Anna Wheeler, Edna Goodfellow—both waiting back home, each probably ready to accept him again when he returned. But this with Luisa, this was serious. The six months and more of trying for a child with Heather was an omen. Something had interceded to save him from that binding tie.

After a few minutes, Bella Pancia got to his feet. He went into the cabin and clattered around amongst the tools, emerging with a pick.

'My task,' he shrugged. 'Giovanni is always concerned

about the well. There are tree roots that must always be kept from growing into the wells. And dead vines.' He smiled and shrugged again. 'And everything else.'

'Can I help you?'

Mario glanced at Luisa, who was picking at a blade of grass. 'It is one man's job. Please relax. You like it here?'

'It's very beautiful,' he replied, but Mario was already heading down the terraces with the pick over his shoulders, and did not hear the automatic tone of Henry's voice.

Henry looked around. Luisa had already gone. He saw her walking in the opposite direction to her father, going into the neighbouring vineyards. How big was Faruggia's task, how long would it take? But Henry didn't care. The mountain breeze was in his hair as he went after Luisa.

She was teasing him, calling him, running amongst the vines while he tripped and nearly fell. But then he caught her and she pulled him down into the dirt, and they made their way under all the vines and the leaves. As they lay on the abundant terrace, grapes hung above their faces; they might have been in some secluded grotto it was so quiet and private and cool.

Luisa took a grape and put it between his lips, and when she took one herself they shared a thought: as in the forest, here they were hidden from everything.

Henry went back to the old shed at the top of Giovanni's side of Bazzio, alone.

'Where is Luisa?' Bella Pancia asked as he returned the pick to its place inside the shed. His face was streaked with dirt and there were drops of water in his moustache from the long drink he had taken at the well.

Yes, Mario Faruggia was fat, Henry told himself, but he suited the part. Like a donkey or a mule—built for sweat and dumb labour.

'I don't know. I haven't seen her for ages. I think she's wandering around.'

'There are sparrows' nests in the orange trees over there. She's probably gone to check on the babies, or she's picking flowers.' He smiled at Henry and flexed an arm. Swinging the pick had been good. It had almost taken his mind off Luisa, but now of course it was all in front of him again.

He sat on the grass and dusted off his trousers. A cord kept them together at the waist and there were small holes at both knees. Slowly he wiped the sweat from his forehead.

The time was now—it could never be better. But his heart started pounding. The people of Piedemonte spoke of his bad blood; perhaps after all, they were correct. *If only there was some way to explain to someone—I wasn't ever meant to stay here; my father had me at the altar too young; my wife with a baby, too young; the new life waiting in Kate's apartment.*

Mario's dirty fingers found the crucifix around his neck. But for Luisa now—

Henry Gill sat down on the grass next to him as Mario's heart pounded away.

'Signore Gill, my daughter Luisa, she is a very good girl.'

Henry stared sharply up toward the horizon.

'I would like to talk to you about a matter, a certain matter.' Mario's voice was hesitant, too soft. His fingers dug at a weed in the grass. 'She is a good girl, but here in Piedemonte—' He didn't know how to go on. The words were wrong, it sounded as if he was trying to sell Henry Gill a donkey or a lorry. If only Kate had been there. In her reasonable voice she could have explained everything. 'Piedemonte is so small, the people are so poor.' He felt he was a refugee begging an indifferent government for sanctuary. 'There is so little for a girl to look forward to—'

For the first time since starting he stole a glance at Henry Gill. Of course it was all wrong! He had been wrong to even think of it, much less say it. Henry Gill's face told the story. Mario's sense of shame was almost complete.

Henry Gill's heart was pounding too. Had it been so obvious?

And if Faruggia knew about them, did Heather as well? He felt the tears of frustration in his eyes.

But in the end—so what? Everything in the world must be for Luisa now, and there was so little time to get it right.

'And the future—I know there is the Signora Gill.' Mario had no idea why he had spoken again. The weeds came away to his blunt fingers and he flicked the barbed leaves aside.

'Stop it, Mr Faruggia. Stop it.' His voice sounded wrong and he cleared his throat. 'There is no need to go on. No need at all. You've made your point, of course, but I want you to know—' Henry stopped. What did he want Faruggia to know that he hadn't already guessed? But it had to all be for Luisa. 'I want you to know that I'll be coming back for your daughter. What there is between us—' But that too was wrong, he couldn't discuss that with the girl's father. 'That's all there is to it. I have a good life in Australia, and you'll be welcome there. I have a little money, so you won't need to be concerned for Luisa about that. I'll admit that I've got a pretty good career as well.'

Henry took a deep breath. He didn't know what else to say. Mario Faruggia was silent and Henry could not bring himself to meet the deep dark eyes. They sat together in the quiet. In the early afternoon light the hills had turned gold and Mt Etna was covered in the horizon's soft glow.

'As you correctly point out, there is Mrs Gill. I'm sorry for that.' His voice was beginning to lose its assured quality. 'But when the time is right and everything has been sorted out, I will be back for Luisa. There is no doubt about that, absolutely none at all.'

He knew he could not continue staring at the hills forever. Henry turned to Mario Faruggia, and when he did he saw that the man was silently weeping. As if for comfort, his filthy workman's hand rested on his breast, over the gold crucifix.

In Piedemonte's small main square, Ezzio Licastro, the town's chief of police, had set up his own television set on top of a sturdy pile of cartons. They ran electric cables from the police station, then because so many people were gathering, Oscar Alanni, the retired avocat, had his son bring the family television set into the square as well. More electric cables were run, and Ezzio Licastro watched with pride from his door as the large and growing group of old townspeople stared up at the twin television screens.

Finally in Piedemonte, this was progress! The force of the media had brought everyone together at last. America would put two men onto the moon's surface and the people of Piedemonte would see it with their own eyes. Licastro called his senior officer—there were only three men stationed in the town—to him. They saluted formally.

'See, Paolo. There is the future. Change will come.'

'Si, Maresciallo!' The officer saluted again.

There was a party atmosphere in the square. Someone had set up a little stand for roasting peanuts and the local parish priest had strung the coloured lights normally reserved for religious festivals through the trees. The coffee shops served cappuccino at a brisk pace to the outdoor tables. People milled and watched the television screens set side by side high up on the cartons, some fought for position, others stood in groups and shook their heads at the impossibility of what was supposed to be happening.

If there was one thing that Ezzio Licastro might have wished for, it was that something a little more scientific had been chosen to be broadcast before the live report of the moon landing. Cartoon characters chased each other over hill and dale, beat each other senseless, came back to life before the confused eyes of Piedemonte.

He continued watching from the doorway of the police station. Down the main street walking toward the square was Luisa Faruggia. Behind her was Signore Faruggia, newly returned from America. People said that he was back to sell the shop and take the profit, and once again leave Luisa to fend for herself.

Well, that was a family matter, it had nothing to do with the police. But Licastro knew what he would do if he suddenly came upon Mario Faruggia one night in a dark, secluded street.

And there was the foreigner who had smashed his car. Licastro wished that there had been some town damage done so that he could have prosecuted the man, but it had only been a stone wall he had driven into and there was no evidence of reckless driving. At least none forthcoming. He watched the three of them, walking in single file as if they were not together. Luisa was waving to friends, and that made him smile. She was a good girl, a wholesome girl, and Licastro had a shy son of twenty.

He looked to the foreigner again, tall and standing out from the crowds in his white shirt. But hadn't he seen the other foreigner a little earlier?

His dark eyes searched through the people standing and milling about the square. Of course, she stood out from the townspeople as well, in her light-coloured skirt and jacket, her light brown hair, her thin face and legs. La Signora Gill, the Australian woman. Ezzio Licastro didn't like the look of these western women. They starved themselves like sparrows, they were so pale, so drawn and so thin, always with something to say. They were good as prostitutes, which they of course enjoyed, but that was all.

He watched la Signora Gill as she talked animatedly to the man she stood with, the small and rotund local doctor who had saved Licastro's son from tuberculosis in 1958. Licastro touched his forefinger to his lips as he watched Dottore de Sica, the last part of the sign of the cross that he always made when seeing the doctor.

His eyes returned to the Australian woman, and as he watched her talking, talking, talking, his lips curled with distaste.

The cartoon characters stopped chasing each other and the picture on both screens became obscure. If people had trouble understanding what had gone on before, that was nothing compared with what happened now.

The pictures and dialogue made no sense. To the Sicilians, the commentators from Rome and Milan who spoke in perfect Italian were barely intelligible. The pictures were nothing. On the screens, white bloated figures came and went, came and went, something round and white was shining out from blackness—but what was it all? The voices of the newsmen tried to tell them it was Americans landing on the moon. Interpreters translated conversations with American scientists—NASA, Houston, Armstrong.

The bloated figures in white were back on the screen. They had great white boots and tubes that went into their heads. Static on the screens followed by more static, incomprehensible languages were being spoken. What was that thing a man was crawling out of—it looked like two Nazi tanks painted white and stacked on top of each other. The slowness of the man's movements was ridiculous!

This was America again!

But Henry Gill was pushing through the crowd. A newsman was speaking with excitement in Italian. Henry strained his ears to hear what was going on but everyone was standing around talking, eating, laughing. He was exhausted from the walk back but he had to see President John F. Kennedy's promise to the world come true.

'Scusi, scusi,' he said over and over again, pushing forward with Mario Faruggia following behind him. Luisa came as well, laughing at her friends, whistling for her dog. It had been a perfect day. She saw her cousin Loretta and gave her a hug and three kisses on the cheek.

And then Henry was right in front of one of the screens, Faruggia beside him. They saw Armstrong emerging from the module, his clumsy feet on the ladder going down to the surface. While others turned away for roasted nuts and coffee, and Ezzio Licastro beat his hand onto his thigh with frustration at

his townspeople, Henry Gill and Mario Faruggia watched the
blurred images and fading pictures.

'That's one small step for a man—'

'Henry! Henry!'

Heather Gill was leading Dottore de Sica by his pudgy hand.
It was easier for the two of them to get to the television screens
for the crowds were thinning even at the most important moment. Heather saw her husband's face as he stared at the pictures with his mouth open. He was like a boy again! She heard
an American voice describing something about sinking an
eighth of an inch into fine powder.

'Henry, Henry! Have you been home yet?'

'No—we just—' But he did not go on or take his eyes from
the screen.

'Henry, this is Doctor de Sica. He speaks English.'

With irritation, Henry finally turned. The reflection of the
screen made his face seem ashen.

'Hello.'

'Signore Gill,' the small fat doctor bowed and nodded. 'Buo-
na sera. I have been taking coffee with your charming wife.'
The man was as pleased as punch and could not stop smiling,
could not stop looking from Henry to Heather and back again.
'Your wife, la Signora Gill has come to me today—'

'Henry, it was impossible to get rid of you!'

Mario Faruggia had now turned from the television as well.
He stared at the doctor.

'La Signora, she has given to me—excuse me please, my English.' He cleared his throat and started again. 'La Signora has
given me the pleasure to announce, and it is with great pleasure
that I do, the results—'

It was as if he might read out some lottery ticket numbers, or
the names of the first three horses in a race. Henry was watching
his wife, her bad skin, her pale face, the lethargy—it all added
up to the same prize.

The little doctor beamed. 'With the family history la Signora has described to me, I would be very surprised if you were not to be blessed with twins. Perhaps not immediately, not the first time of course—'

Henry Gill said nothing. He looked back to the television screen, at the imperfect images of a barren waste now carrying two human lives. The speakers crackled, the pictures faded. Up behind the television sets, Mt Etna cast a red glow into the night sky.

Henry and Mario Faruggia heard Luisa calling. She was crouched down and whistling gently for her grey dusty dog. Nosing into a discarded piece of bread soaked with olive oil, it wagged its tail but refused to come.

FORGETFUL FINGERS ON THE
G STRING

1 A Witch

Naked by the glass, on the day she had been looking forward to for two years and more—which by happenstance was the tenth anniversary of the American Woodstock Music Festival—Emma set about making herself up layer by layer.

Early morning summer sunshine fell across the patterned quilt of her single bed as Triple Zed's sardonic breakfast shift announcer played this song for the occasion:

> This ain't the Garden of Eden
> There ain't no angels above
> And things ain't what they're supposed to be
> And this ain't the Summer of Love.

The music was low as if it might disturb others in the house, but the truth was that Emma had lived alone in her guardian's rambling old colonial ever since he had first decided to go backpacking across Europe.

From her window overlooking the street Emma watched the small crowd she would soon join at the number 177 bus stop. She slid tight jeans over her tightly muscled bottom, automatically thinking: eight kilometres jogging five days out of seven, fifty Olympic swimming laps nine days out of fourteen.

Her legs were long, there was firm definition in her biceps, and the symmetrical lines of muscle were clear in her abdomen.

But when Emma buttoned a white shirt over her small breasts, their points seemed to stare back at her from out of the clean glass of the closet's full-length mirror. Hard, long, curious, unloved—these were the words which came into her mind.

Still, it was the great Summer of Love ten years earlier that was most in her thoughts, and would have been anyway with or without the anniversary. For the bolt out of the blue had arrived only the day before: 'Emma flt 226 Luft 10.20am tomorrow, Your Faithful Guardian'.

No wonder then that in these recent years of school and university there had only been the occasional boy to grope her here and prod her there and bore her senseless with sweaty palms and seas of Old Spice.

But her guardian, Saul Bellman—a picture of him was creased into a corner of the long mirror's glass—was something else, all blue eyes and golden-brown hair that ended in ringlets at his shoulders.

The photo was an old one, taken in 1969 when Saul had been playing in his flower-power band, several years before her parents had been killed and he had shown his true friendship for them by becoming her legal guardian.

Emma was now six months from turning twenty; when one day she had realised her affection for Saul was real and deep and not the product of some prepubescent fantasy, she had experienced a sense of relief.

In essence, all that was missing was Saul himself.

There was so much to tell him: her dates with adolescent boys too nervous to hold her hand; the trendy young punks at university dances who broke the skin on their wrists with glass and led their loved ones around on spiked dog collars; the reviewer at Triple Zed whom she had spent a night with and who the next day had sent her a gift-wrapped leather G-string.

A child of Woodstock, Saul would understand this poverty of spirit Emma saw everywhere. A leather G-string—to some people this was love!

Emma looked through her window at the people waiting at the bus stop and reflected on the two years and more without

Saul. Now that he was returning the loneliness she had felt in all that time was unimportant. She brushed her hair vigorously, eager to run from the house and catch her first bus connection to Brisbane's tiny international airport.

'But the people from flight 226, you mean they've even been through Customs?' Emma asked, shaking her head with disbelief at the unexpected efficiency of the world travel system. Saul's Lufthansa flight had arrived a full two and a half hours ahead of schedule. What had it been—a tail-wind like a typhoon, a flight captain with a girlfriend in Brisbane and a tremendous Aryan urge to see her?

'Yes, everyone is quite through. May I suggest that it is wise to reconfirm flight details at least—'

'But I did!'

The attendant smiled politely, inwardly counting the queue of roughly twenty-five fidgeting behind Emma.

'If you would just move aside.'

Emma wandered up and down the busy terminal. She hadn't been there to greet him—what must poor Saul have thought! Her eyes sought out every tall, thin man with long hair and golden ringlets, of which there were none.

She sat down heavily in the rows of seats facing the Customs' doors; nothing but Asians and nobly nosed Greeks emerged. Her legs were straight out in front of her, her feet resting on the butt of her heels so that the toes of her shoes pointed toward the ceiling.

Trying to gather her thoughts, Emma watched the steel doors slide irregularly open and shut, spilling passengers greasy with long distance travel out into the waiting arms of loved ones.

There was a tall, handsome Levantine pushing a massive trolley of suitcases marked with stickers of 'Roma' and 'Milano'. Wide-lapelled white shirt open to the belly button, a heavy gold chain buried deep in the forest of his chest, tight black trousers with a constricting waistband that came right up to the ribs.

A blonde with an enormous round behind pushed through the restlessly waiting crowd and threw her arms around the thick neck. In front of everyone the two were face-on-face; Emma watched the tip of a pink tongue join with another.

Gross-out!

But after all, that was everything love had become, wasn't it?

She resolutely clicked open her small change purse and considered the few silver coins. The present Emma had purchased for Saul after receiving the telegram had well and truly cleaned out her resources. There hadn't been enough for a taxi to the airport, there certainly wasn't enough for a quick ride home. Even a telephone call to see if he had arrived at the house would leave her short for the bus trips home.

It had cost her dearly, that second-hand Ovation electric six string. Emma imagined presenting him with it—Welcome Home, Saul! She would tell him all about how she had gone into the shop and used her own tool-kit to pull the guitar apart before buying it. How she had found serious faults and bartered the price down.

And God, what faults—a veritable musical death trap hanging in a shop front window! She'd only had a little time to fix the bugs that could have given an unsuspecting musician an almighty wallop from the mains. Emma had replaced the burnt-black wiring before going to bed; getting up early in the morning she had fitted a proper new pick-up the way her father had shown her when she was still only ten years of age. And polished the whole thing with natural beeswax until you could see your reflection in the wood panelling.

Still, even at fifty dollars less—Emma snapped the purse shut. Unintelligible announcements were being made over the PA system. She looked at her watch and checked a crumpled bus timetable.

Late again, Emma ran out into the hot day for the distant airport bus service.

The big old house was still and quiet at midday when Emma arrived, breathless and perspiring, fumbling with the front door key. She stopped herself and took a deep breath, straightened her hair, bit her bottom lip, entered the house.

And waited in the front room. The house seemed empty, dark, silent.

The hallway was long and when her eye became accustomed to the dimness she saw the suitcase propped against the wall, some hand luggage beside it, a brown leather jacket discarded on the floor. With the darkness Saul's leather coat looked like a great family pet lying in wait.

She picked the jacket up and pressed the old leather to her cheek; the scent of it was all Saul. A book fell out of an inside pocket and she caught it before it hit the floor. A dog-eared old copy of Ian Fleming's *You Only Live Twice*. Emma smiled at this.

He was lying down in his bedroom, of course. Emma breathed a great sigh, eased the bedroom door open.

'Saul?' The door opened on quiet hinges. 'Saul?' She smiled toward the crumpled mess of the bed—and saw the four white feet sticking out from the sheets at the base of his old four-poster.

The door shut with a thud. Emma backed herself to the hallway wall from where it seemed there was no place left to go.

'Emma? Is that you, Emma?' a voice said, then with greater determination, 'Emma, just give me a minute!' A woman's low voice complained with sleeplessness. From the bedroom Saul was saying loudly, 'How are you, Emma? Couldn't make it to the airport—lectures at uni, I bet. No matter! Flight early, couldn't believe it. Tried to ring you here but no answer. Look, I'm just— give me a minute!'

The other voice became more persistent; with disbelief Emma realised that sleeplessness had nothing to do with the way it sounded.

After so long—this?

Emma wanted to run from the house with her hands over

her ears. Instead, she escaped to the kitchen and put the kettle onto the stove, found matches and dropped them, found tea and spilled it, switched the gas on and off, went to the television and turned 'The Mike Walsh Show' on and off as well.

When footsteps finally came down the corridor Emma was sitting at the kitchen table, quietly waiting for the kettle to boil. 'Tea?' she inwardly told herself to ask as carefully she would butter some white bread. Composure—of all things, composure. 'Tea?' she attempted in her mind. 'White? With or without?'

A shadow preceded the footsteps into the kitchen and her heart missed a beat.

But it wasn't Saul at all, only a spindly matchstick of a— what? Over six feet tall in tight black jeans and a tight black T-shirt and with black mascara caked around the eyes. Cheeks gaunt and pale, hair dyed too black to look natural.

'Hello, love,' it spoke.

Emma stared. A witch!

'I'm Irene, you must be Emma. Saulie's told me so much about you I feel like I know you already.' A witch with a Lon-doner's common accent!

Emma was frozen where she sat, her hands clasped before her as if they were a fixture of the table.

'You know the flights were a disaster until Singapore where a new crew came on board,' the horrible voice continued with what might have been friendliness, 'and then we made such good time none of us could believe it, is that tea, love?' The witch seemed to talk without any human need to draw breath. 'Saulie will just love to have some and I'll have a cup too if there's any left over, you know I don't mind if you don't use a strainer, Lord bless my mum she always said the tea leaves were good for your vitals though that's rubbish you know, you just get the taste for it, that's all. Give us your hand, Emma, and let's do the formal thing!'

Emma looked up into the black bloodshot eyes, watched

the lips that smiled under black lipstick. Her hand went into a damp skeleton's grasp. As Black-Eyed Irene then helped herself to the teapot, Emma carefully wiped her hand under the table. Irene's palm had been greasy with—what?—sweat, or Saul?

'Saulie's so proud of you, you know Emma, your running and your swimming and the way you do with your studies. God, you're a fit-looking thing, aren't you? I used to like netball myself in the old days before the music thing happened but the gigs keep me fit now, you know what I mean of course, don't you love? Talk about a wonderful house!'

Emma thought she must try and speak, but was pessimistic about how anything she said might sound. Perhaps—Oh, you're a musician? but heavy footfalls thudded down the polished timber floor of the hallway toward the kitchen door.

Finally!

It wasn't Saul either, but some heavy-set man, the male twin of the witch Irene. Stovepipe black jeans torn and riddled with badges and safety pins, the jeans open at the front to accommodate a huge belly which pushed against a thin black T-shirt just like the one Black-Eyed Irene wore. More badges there. Thin white arms hanging from the barrel of his torso, skinny legs supporting it all, a great football of a head topped with a crew-cut of hair dyed too-black. A huge, welcoming, all-embracing grin that showed perfect white teeth.

Emma felt the beginnings of panic—who were these side-show freaks in her house?

'Emma darling!'

And bright unchanged blue eyes.

Emma's mouth was open. A rush of air like sweet sixties music filled her ears. As she hadn't done since kindergarten when she had jagged her foot on a rusty nail and the blood had refused to stop flowing, Emma slumped sideways in a dead faint.

It was much later, dinner time in fact. The three of them had rested the afternoon through, Saul and the witch Irene in his bedroom, Emma huddled alone across her narrow bed. She had kept the radio on to cover anything untoward that might have come from Saul's room. To complete her misery, every hour Triple Zed played sardonic homages to their long-haired predecessors at Woodstock. Flowers in gun barrels, long hair, communal nudity in swimming holes.

Only to end in this!

Emma dozed, shivered, woke to the picture of Saul pressed into the corner of her long mirror. Saul as he had been and should still have been.

It was past seven and there was the cloying odour of garlic in the air. Emma pushed herself from the bed and straightened her hair. Her face in the mirror was pale. The small photo of Saul was all blue eyes and golden ringlets—an Adonis. She forced herself out into the kitchen and there the Adonis stood chopping a capsicum, his back to her.

Unlike the wasted punks he somehow seemed to be emulating, Saul's great behind tested the seams of his jeans, his belly was all blubber. A sack of potatoes falling from a truck held more shape.

Garlic fried in an electric pan as he swiftly diced the capsicum, chopped an onion, quartered juicy tomatoes. From a ceramic goblet she watched him throw back a cup of flagon claret with a great gulp. Two badges on his back pocket read 'Clash Rule' and 'Fuck Off'.

Emma quietly sat down at the kitchen table. Her palms were damp and the smell of the garlic cooking in oil made her stomach churn. Saul turned from his work.

'Emma darling, there you are! Hungry? Or still feeling off-colour? God, you gave me such a fright this afternoon. I thought you were going to sleep the whole day. When I took you to your room you were completely away with it. You haven't been studying and training too hard, have you? Or is it your period playing up? You're still a little pale but some spaghetti will cheer you up, won't it? Irene's asleep, the poor thing. There are those who really shouldn't travel. Like some wines.'

He filled the cheap goblet from the flagon and swallowed it down, making a face, then he went to Emma and put his incongruously thin arms around her. Saul's wet lips kissed her cheek and in spite of everything, the kiss made her blush. Saul stepped back and studied her the way one might study a painting in a gallery. 'A little pale,' he said with a smile, 'but so pretty. Don't you agree?'

Emma looked back at him. What lines she remembered in his face were gone, pushed out, puffed out by his new weight.

Saul might have understood her expression for he looked away and went back to his cutting board, wielding the sharp kitchen knife with authority. Another innovation—the Saul she remembered had been lost in the kitchen, unless there were lentils to boil.

'Well Emma, we've got a lot of catching up to do, that's for sure. Your studies?'

'Yes, yes, they're fine,' she managed to say, words drying up even as she thought them. 'What ... what have you been doing?'

'Oh, it's been a great old time,' he replied looking back and giving her a wink. Saul found oregano and pepper, some minced chillies. Finally he went on: 'What I've been doing is—changing. As you can see.' He turned for her reaction, then helped himself from the flagon. 'Giving myself a new lease on life. A new beginning, so to speak. What do you think of that?'

Hardly anything!

When he wasn't looking Emma closed her eyes. It was his voice, a little more authoritative but still gentle, still with that sweetness.

'You know, Emma, I thought I was through. Hit forty, can you imagine it? Me—forty! Slammed into it. You can't understand what that's like. Everything for me was in the past, back in the silly sixties. My band, the old songs, Jesus! What was I supposed to do now, become a producer, a manager? Start my own record label? Out of what—the metaphysics of Woodstock? And there were generations of kids and new music just coming and going and I was left behind with the old farts.'

Saul turned to Emma for a moment, his eyes actually shining.

But he's dying to tell me all this! Emma realised with crawling skin. In her mind there was a picture of the old Saul breaking out of the fat cocoon of the new, a persistent image. Ha-ha, tricked you, Emma—but it didn't happen.

'And then I landed in London and the whole scene there was turning the world on its head. You know what I mean! I was holed up in Earls Court with all the other Aussies, broke, hopeless. A job here and a job there. Playing guitar in wine bars. Woody Guthrie, Simon and Garfunkel, big deal. What a yawn. And then I saw Irene's band playing in the same pub where I was recycling the old standards. You know what Irene and her friends did? They trashed the place, blew it apart, set fire to the stage and to their instruments. Fire! Can you believe it? The crowd went wild, the atmosphere was incredible. I had to meet this woman! They didn't even call the police. It was the same all over London, the kids were taking over with their guitars. Your parents and I had the Summer of Love—this was the Winter of Hate! And Irene, when I met her, I thought she'd be the angriest thing on the planet. And look at her—a bona fide English Rose. Did my life change? On the spot!'

He wanted Emma to be smiling with him but found nothing in her eyes.

'I was all wrong you know, crazy with 1969, lost in the new world. Irene and I put together a band and started writing. We played all the crappy pubs and the rage came right out of me. Fantastic stuff, Emma. And the kids took me to their hearts. Look at me, over forty and overweight and they danced to the music right with us. But London's full of people like Irene and me, there are too many for us to make a real impression. So that's why we're here.'

'That's why?'

'What do you think, Emma? Do you think I'll be able to get it together? We want to set a few Aussie pubs on fire, shake the whole place up. I know I'm older but I'm not over the hill. I know I'm a few pounds heavier but I've got more energy than I've ever had. More than I know what to do with. That Irene—' He shook himself back to reality. 'Look at this sauce,' Saul said, staring into the pan. 'Good and thick, got a kick. I'm alive again and everyone's going to know about it. Triple Zed too, it's so bloody exciting. Tell me what you really think, Emma.'

He turned to the kitchen table; the chair was pushed away, empty. In the deep electric pan the rich red sauce was bubbling.

'Emma?'

It was with difficulty that Emma made herself sit at the dinner table with Saul and Irene and watch them demolish the huge bowl of spaghetti. She ate little and excused herself quickly, going to her room and trying to reconcile this new spaghetti-sucking Saul with the Saul pressed into the corner of the mirror. The radio was on softly, again the announcers played Country Joe and the Fish to ridicule Woodstock's anniversary.

She worked backwards: the fiftieth anniversary was gold, twenty-fifth was silver. What was the tenth? She racked her brain and then it came to her. It was tin.

Bloody ironic.

For a while Emma watched through her window the darkness outside. She remembered the dinner conversation taking place around her while she had remained quiet and subdued, reduced to being only a third of the household rather than the whole, a rapidly diminishing third at that.

'There's Steve, great drummer but likes a drink. Or Raymond. And there's Wally too. But I tell you what, Irene, I might just give the old hands a miss altogether. And if they cry when we make it big with younger guys, well it'll just be sparrow's tears, do you get what I mean? Insignificant. We'll find some young musicians with chips on their shoulders, kids with something to prove, Emma's age. We can even have our practices here. Shit, we could all live here, the place is big enough. We'll have a sixties commune of punks. What a laugh! What do you say?'

And just what had Irene said, sauce streaked across her pasty cheek like a bloodstain on a chalkboard?

'Saulie, it's perfect. Just perfect.'

Emma now buried her head under her pillow.

It was much later that there came a tapping on her door. 'You're awake, aren't you, Emma?' Saul asked from behind it.

Just in time, she propped herself up on the pillow holding the first book her hand had landed upon.

'Studying, hey? You're a good girl, Emma, but don't overdo it. I'm just a bit worried about you, you know. Are you feeling okay? You're still pale as anything. I would have thought all that swimming and running would have made you brown as a berry. Didn't I give you that book?'

He came further into the room and sat on the edge of her bed.

'For my last birthday before you left.'

'So I did, so I did. I thought it was so great at the time. Somerset Maugham, king of the bloody old farts. Larry Darrell searching for spirituality.' He smiled ruefully, looking at the cover. Emma watched him. Saul was huge, the room was stuffed with his vast presence. He seemed to be smiling at himself as much as at Larry Darrell. 'Been there, done that, eh Emma?'

Saul gazed around at her shelves and Emma felt passive, receptive to anything he might say or do.

'Evelyn Waugh, queen of the private school pansies. And Graham Greene, tired old men wandering under grey skies. Or something like that.'

'I saw you were reading a James Bond book.'

'Ian Fleming! *You Only Live Twice.* I'm up to the part with that Japanese saying, "sparrow's tears". Wonderful expression, only the Japanese could have thought of something that sums things up so perfectly. I've been reading Fleming's books since I was fifteen. Did you know that, Emma? Maybe you thought I was always a hippie. Anyway,' he said, bending to kiss her forehead, 'I think it's time you called it a night. Irene's crashed already, I told you she doesn't travel. It's been a big day. I'm a little bushed myself.'

'Did you miss me?' Emma asked quietly. Out of the corner of her eye she saw the guitar she had bought for Saul propped against a wall in the corner.

'All that time?' His hand went to the hair over her brow, gently smoothed it back. The touch of his fingertips always made her blush. She stared up into the moon of his face. 'Of course I did.'

Emma reached up and took his hand, brought it to her lips and kissed his palm. Even with everything—those blue eyes! The time for being complaisant was over. She felt his tenderness for her, felt his look go right through her all the way down to her toes. She couldn't help herself and she couldn't stop herself—the dream had been two years and more in the making.

Emma turned his hand against her mouth.

Saul noticed the old snapshot pressed into the closet's full-length mirror as Emma took his index finger between her lips and touched its tip with her tongue.

2 Bondo-san Says ...

Emma had to look twice at the mourner who brought her a hot cup of tea. Irene in a new black outfit of jeans and shirt sat smiling at the edge of her bed, just as Saul had done the night before. Emma hadn't slept well, thinking all night that at this moment or the next Saul might come to her room.

But how could he have with this witch watching him like a hawk?

It was late morning.

Emma drew the sheet up to her chin and focused on the witch, the skinny stovepipe frame perfectly out of balance with the heavy breasts pushing against her black shirt.

And black appraising eyes—yes, Irene was a mourner, an elegist of the apocalypse.

'White without, that's how Saul said you take your tea. He was very clear about that. He wanted to bring it to you himself but I told him to have a lie in. You must have classes today?'

'No, not today.' This was a lie for Thursday was the busiest day of her week. 'It's free.'

'Lucky you then. You wouldn't need classes anyway, Saul says you're that bright. Anyway, you'll have the place to yourself, Emma.' Irene seemed more relaxed than she'd been the day before, today she spoke and drew breath as a human does. 'Saul wants to let his old friends know he's back. I wonder how they'll react! I hope no one makes a fuss about joining the new band, but Saul's made up his mind to use young musicians so that's that. Mind, I wouldn't want to cross Saulie today. He's in a mood!'

'Yes?' Emma's interest started to rise. 'A mood?'

'I've never seen him like this,' Irene said quickly, a horrified half-smile twitching her lips. 'Except when we're playing to a crowd. It must be the flying, you know, at his age and all that. Disorientation. He tossed and turned all night and this morning he nearly bit my head off. Not a kind word.'

Emma looked closely at Irene. Was that a tear somewhere behind the heavy mascara? 'Yes?'

But Irene would not go on. Emma watched with mounting horror as the fat tear blended with the eye-liner and made a charcoal streak down the white powdered face.

She remembered what Saul had said of the Japanese. This then was truly it—the inconsequential tears of an English sparrow.

Everything was going to work out all right after all, Emma told herself. Now that he knew of her feelings for him, Saul had tossed and turned all night. They just had to get this Black-Eyed Irene back to the London pubs—somehow. Emma needed to speak to Saul.

She held the sheet tightly under her chin. 'Irene, I wonder if you could do me a favour, I mean, would you mind?'

'What's that, love?' The dark streak was like clown's make-up on Irene's cheek. Emma stared at it as she might have stared at a wound.

'You know I wasn't well yesterday, I need some—' She couldn't bring herself to say the word to the witch. 'Things.'

'You can have some of mine. I've always got plenty.'

'Oh no, I need my special kind.'

'Well, mine will be enough until—'

'Please, Irene.' Emma tried her best to look desperate and lost. 'I'm very uncomfortable. The shop's down the road and they sell chamomile tea as well, which really helps me on days like this. And could you get me the paper, and some milk too? It would be such a help.'

Of course the witch would help. She even gave Emma a brief hug before leaving the room.

Emma waited until she heard Irene's footsteps go down the corridor and the sound of the front door falling shut, then she pulled on her white bathrobe and checked her face in the mirror.

He was in his bedroom.

Just now rising, Saul sat on the edge of the old four-poster trying to do up the front of his jeans. He sucked in his stomach to no avail and saw Emma standing in the doorway. Saul's feet were white and bare, his chest and shoulders were matted with hair. Emma had never seen him so naked.

'Gets harder and harder to do these up,' he laughed, but he was trying to read the expression on Emma's face. 'The price of age for Grandfather Punk. It's what gives me away. I really would like to tell people I'm younger.'

'You don't look a day over thirty.'

Saul made a face. 'Tell Irene to get some coffee on.'

'She's gone out.'

'Oh?' And a little spark of worry creased the flat brow.

Emma came in with small steps, Japanese style. In the semi-darkness of the bedroom's undrawn curtains her dressing robe could have been a kimono. Her smile too could have been that of one of the girls from the respectable geisha houses Saul had frequented when in Tokyo at the start of his backpackers trek. He remembered the polite, ivory-skinned Japanese girls, the one geisha house in particular just off the Ginza, the pillow book they had given him as a memento. Just like James Bond in *You Only Live Twice*. What had Bondo-san's girlfriend been called?

Emma sat beside him on the bed. He couldn't bring himself to look at her face when her warm hand closed over his. She didn't speak; her shyness touched him deeply. Saul was aware of his heartbeat. Before the Age of Blubber—as he called it—he would have been able to see his heart moving in his chest.

But this couldn't really be.

Saul stared straight ahead, afraid to speak and afraid to move, studying the cheap panelling of his wardrobe as if it were a work of great intricacy. Little Emma!

Her chin was so low it almost touched the soft fabric tightly crossed around her chest. 'I love you, Saul,' Emma spoke as quietly as a thought. She kissed him, the warm sweet mouth pressed to his neck just above the shoulder. Emma!

And she was gone from the room and Irene was bawling down the corridor, 'Do you know how hard it is to explain what chamomile tea is to bloody Greeks! Emma, I thought you said they kept it there at that shop? Never bloody heard of the stuff, I had to go all the way down the street to the supermarket!'

But Saul's thoughts were, if anything, Japanese. Emma's robe, the small steps, the shyness. He remembered the name of Bondo-san's Japanese girlfriend: Kissy Suzuki.

Tonight, when he had the chance, he would unpack the old dog-eared pillow book.

The guitar wasn't plugged into the wall socket or the small amplifier, and the strumming only sounded thin and muted. Still, Emma watched Irene's deft fingers on the fretboard, the complex jazz progressions. Emma envied the light touch and the ease with which the long fingers handled the strings. She had just come out of the shower and there Irene had been, sitting in Emma's room helping herself to Saul's Welcome Home gift.

'Hope you don't mind, I didn't think you would, I saw it this morning when I brought you your tea. Saul's still in his mood. Had to get away from him for a minute. But we'll be off to see his friends soon, then the house is all yours.' Irene put the instrument back where she had found it. 'Our equipment's still on the way. By ship, it will take forever. Not that we've got all that much. Is it yours?'

'Yes,' Emma said without hesitation.

The pale black-eyed face of the witch looked up at her. Sometime during the morning Irene had discovered the charcoal mark and had rubbed fresh powder into her cheeks. Perhaps it was the light in the room, but for the first time Emma saw why Irene kept her face so powdered: the cheeks were heavily pockmarked and ugly under the make-up.

Like a pineapple, Emma thought, Irene's face. And her legs as long and thin as string beans. Her chest like rock melons. How could Emma be rid of her quickly?

'So, do you mind then, Emma love, do you mind if I play your guitar every now and then? I like to keep in practice you know, I won't even plug it in.'

'No, no, you can any time you want. Here.' Emma showed her the small practice amplifier she kept in her cupboard, threw the leads and electric plugs down beside the guitar. 'There's all you need. Just plug it all together when you feel like it.' Emma wondered if her smile looked as insincere as it felt, whether the words sounded as stale as they tasted.

'Is your period better now?'

Emma forced the smile to stay on her face. 'Yes thanks.'

'I might try some of that herbal tea myself. I bet it's very soothing. Saul could use some too. Especially today. He's a cat on a hot tin roof, have you noticed yet? I can't even look at him without getting my arse kicked—metaphysically speaking.' Irene went to the guitar again and ran her fingers over the neck. 'I'll leave you be. Beautiful strings you've got on this.'

Emma thought: For Saul, not you.

Alone in her room, Emma went to the mirror and looked at Saul's photo, thinking of him at his bedside with her hand over his. For that and more, what would she do?

The question was underscored just thirty minutes later when Saul and Irene were leaving the house. The midday sunshine was hot. Saul and Irene—twins in their black—were already sweltering.

'I'll make dinner tonight,' Emma said.

'You're better then?'

'Much better.'

'Hang on,' Irene spoke. 'I've forgotten my purse.'

As Irene went back into the house Saul pulled Emma to him. His arms were damp and his belly pressed into her chest.

'Emma,' he said, and that was all.

Irene soon returned and Saul gave her a curt sidelong glance. 'Got it,' she tried to say with enthusiasm.

'About bloody time.'

'All right!' Hating each other, both of them crossed the street. Emma watched until they were nothing more than smudges in the shimmering heat.

It was cooler in the house and she turned on the few ceiling fans to get the air moving. She wanted to sit and think about nothing but Saul, but there was an assignment that needed writing. Emma was as fastidious with her work as she was with her running and swimming schedules. There had never been a late assignment, never a piece of work that fell below her usual high standard. Emma liked to think of it in that way: Her Usual High Standard.

So she sat at her desk and headed a page with the topic:

Spirituality and Zen in the Work of W. Somerset
Maugham

But without real thought a word appeared in bright blue
ink on the ruled page of her note book:

arsenic

Emma considered this. In the evening meal? Pasta, mush-
rooms, garlic and arsenic? Or any poison—rat poison for
instance?

She looked around her bookshelves for a more aesthetic
means of murder, something literary. But her writers seemed to
all fall back on the old standards: a bullet in a vital place, deadly
poison in a meal or drink, a tight cord around the throat when
least expected. Or some precious heavy icon brought down
upon a skull—a leaden Maltese falcon for instance, though she
couldn't remember if any of Dashiell Hammett's characters had
met their maker in that way.

Emma screwed up the wasted page and started another.

Spirituality and Zen in the ...

She swivelled her chair so that she could look at the old
photo of Saul.

But after all, wasn't that exactly it? Wasn't Saul still looking
for enlightenment, just as he and all the others had done in the
sixties? This new need of his for rebirth and meaning—maybe
nothing was different in him at all, perhaps it was just that Irene
had taken Saul in the wrong direction.

Saul was Larry Darrell, not Sid Vicious. He was Jay Gatsby,
Dick Diver, Monroe Stahr—not Rat Scabies or Johnny Rotten
or Stiv Bators.

And so it was even more imperative to get him away from the witch. Arsenic, strangulation—how appropriate!

Unwilling to concentrate on Somerset Maugham, Emma went to the kitchen and made herself a health sandwich: brown bread, lettuce, tomato, bean sprouts and homemade relish. She put the kettle on for some chamomile tea, and as she waited for the water to boil she opened a large kitchen drawer and studied the many cooking utensils. They were endlessly fascinating.

A long serrated bread knife, a meat tenderiser, a heavy rolling pin, an electric meat carver. Emma laid them out on the counter like a totem, adding the short peeling knife and something sharp that might have been meant for sticking pigs. How had that been added to the kitchen?

From another cupboard she took a heavy duty garbage bag—beware of suffocation—and pressed it flat onto the kitchen table. All that was missing was a ball of twine to tighten the thick bag at the throat. Emma studied the options: so many from just one small kitchen!

But far down the hallway she heard the front door open and slam shut. The kettle was whistling; she dropped her sandwich in the haste of stuffing everything back into the drawers. Except for the big bag spread flat and neat on the kitchen table. Emma lunged for it.

When Irene came tearfully into the kitchen she found Emma collecting kitchen scraps into a heavy duty black garbage bag.

Emma tried to make her voice full of friendly surprise—'Oh hi, Irene'—busying herself with rubbish that wasn't there. It was a moment before she saw the mascara running down Irene's powdered cheeks.

'What—'

'It's Saul, it's Saul, I just can't get over him today! It's as if he's decided that he hates me, he keeps saying the most horrible things. Today he's—' and in a moment Emma found herself giving comfort to the thin bony shoulders of her bête noire. Mascara came off on the breast of the bathrobe she still wore; she held the gawky frame awkwardly, the only way it was possible to hold Irene.

Soon, the black eyes looked at her. 'Thank you, I'm all right. I just couldn't bear to be with Saul another minute so I left him to his friends. He can have them. I've got it together now.' Emma passed her a clean tissue but it only smudged the caked mascara more. Now Irene's eyes looked as bruised as those of a weary boxer.

'Maybe you should take it easy today,' she found herself saying. 'You know, stay in bed with the papers and the fan on. You've probably still got a bit of jet lag. Saul too—I'm sure that's all that's wrong with him.'

'That's what I thought,' Irene said, rubbing a hand around the close-cropped dyed-black hair of her scalp. 'But I'm not sure. There's something wrong with him. I know there's something going on.' For a moment the thin shoulders were shaking. 'I wish I could just go away.'

Emma's eyes widened. Yes!

'But I've been doing that all my life with men. Not this time.' Irene wiped her eyes with the tissue, blew her nose. 'Not this time, not with Saul. I'm not going to run away from him. Saul and I are forever, you know, that's how it is. Let me play your guitar for a while, Emma?'

'Sure,' Emma said with regret. 'You know where it is.'

Emma considered their triangle: two women and a man, the hub of many a little suburban tragedy. She watched as Irene blew her nose loudly, then the lanky figure took her into her arms again. Another hug—since Saul's return from overseas Emma had had more physical contact from her enemy than from the man she loved.

Irene gave a rueful smile as she left the kitchen.

Water boiled, Emma made the tea in a Chinese pot. But to feel such sympathy for her rival—in a minute she would bring a cup of chamomile tea to Irene, weak and milky as the English were known to like it. Emma thought of the recent kitchen killing inventory with vague disquiet.

'Do you mind if I plug the amplifier in?' Irene's voice called from the hallway.

'No, go ahead, I'm not studying for a while. Just plug it all in'—Emma couldn't help but smile—'and rock'n'roll.'

Irene was quiet now. Emma heard the vague sounds of Irene taking the small practice amplifier out of the bedroom clothes closet. She listened, thinking: That witch, in my room, playing Saul's guitar, rummaging through my things.

Yet somehow the thought lacked its familiar edge.

She poured the tea into two mugs. One said 'Kiss me I'm Sexy' and the other 'World's Greatest Dag'. So out of place in this big old house, where had they come from? She remembered the twin badges on Saul's black jeans—'Clash Rule', 'Fuck Off'—and they seemed similarly out of place. Her hand was shaking slightly. Why?

Irene was in Emma's room, amongst her things, at home. Emma paused with the milk carton in her hand, realised that she felt no enmity toward Irene, none at all. None of it was left; all that seemed important were the thin shoulders shaking, the comfort she had been able to give.

The guitar meant for Saul would bring Irene some solace. Emma wondered at the irony of such a thought, wondered too at the curious magnanimity of the human heart.

And found herself also wondering about the guitar. Those damaged wires inside, the surprised look on the second-hand dealer's face when she had expertly used a small screwdriver to inspect the electricals under the guitar's power plate.

There had been a huge hairy wart above one of the dealer's eyebrows; she had used a lot of furniture wax to get the instrument to shine. Emma sipped the tea. It was weak, the herbal brew went badly with so much milk. Well, it was supposed to be to make Irene feel better. She took both cups and walked around the kitchen counter, thinking that she would ask Irene to play the deft jazz progressions again.

Emma stopped.

The haste and excitement and expense in the second-hand shop, then later in the night when she had repaired the bared wires in the guitar, the same haste and excitement. Emma tried to picture her hands as she had worked with the pliers and screwdriver. They had been shaking—such an extravagant present for Saul! Emma's hands shook now. The bared earth wire, the others burnt black. She had done everything correctly, hadn't she?

Oh dear.

'Irene?' she called from the kitchen doorway, both mugs of tea in her hands. Even to her own ears her voice sounded tentative. She looked down to the breast of her bathrobe. Irene's mascara was smeared there.

Phut!

Just before the lights went out and the ceiling fan slowed, there was that mildly ineffectual bang. A gust of acrid smoke drifted lazily from the open bedroom doorway into the corridor.

Still holding the twin cups of weak tea, Emma watched the dark little cloud of smoke float slowly up toward the high panelled ceilings.

'Irene?'

Much later, Emma had herself together enough to replace the blown fuse in the switchboard. She washed the dirty plates in the sink and swept the kitchen floor, she ran the vacuum cleaner around the lounge-room carpet for a bit then lost interest. She had another shower, this one long and cold, and changed into jeans and a clean shirt. When Saul's heavy footsteps were in the hallway she was sitting at the kitchen table, the Somerset Maugham assignment almost completed to first draft.

Emma looked down at her close, precise script with pride.

'Have you seen Irene?' Saul asked sourly, hot and perspiring in his close-fitting black.

'No.' She tried to think of something else to say but there seemed to be nothing.

'She won't be back,' he said. 'I bet she won't. Oh, for her stuff, sure. But she's no stayer you know, that one's had a list of love affairs longer than your arm.' Saul put his hands on his hips and shook his head. 'Those jerks I went to see.' He seemed agitated, as if many things in his life were not going well. Emma imagined his old friends from the sixties still with their long hair and some still attached to their beads, now confronted with the new Saul. What would they have thought?

But he was gone after a long stare in the silence, a stare that Emma felt to the points of her toes. Then she heard the shower running.

Carefully and calmly she finished the assignment, drawing a neat double line under the final sentence and annotating the last page with the precise word count. She put her books aside and waited.

'Emma.'

His voice called her from the main bedroom. In a moment she was there as he lay spread-eagled across the bed, huge and damp in his large blue bath towel. Saul's eyes, the colour of the towel—she took him in completely. There were drops of water hidden like diamonds amongst the matted hair of his shoulders and chest.

In his hands he held a hardcover book like the large format art books of Gauguin and Paul Klee and Kandinsky she liked to collect.

'It's something I picked up in Tokyo, Emma. It's called a pillow book. Japanese couples use them. I bought it in a place called the Happy Shop. The Happy Shop,' he smiled. 'Do you want to know how I got onto it? From *You Only Live Twice*, of all things. At the end of the book Bondo-san has amnesia and no, you know, desire. He thinks he's a Jap named Taro Todoroki, his girlfriend is Kissy Suzuki.' Saul laughed quietly, glancing at Emma and feeling mild disappointment that she wasn't in her kimono-style bathrobe. 'She buys the book from a sex merchant for Bondo-san, to get him kick-started. Maybe all Japanese couples need a kick-start, huh? I've always wanted one of these.' He looked up at her with the same kind of shyness he had felt when he had been with the demure Japanese girls of the geisha house.

Emma was so pretty—even as a child she had been beautiful—and now she had let him know with certainty that she wanted to be with him. Irene was insignificant in this new situation. He hoped she would come for her things quickly, within the next couple of days, then the memory of her would go just as quickly.

Emma saw the inscribed pornographic photos as Saul flicked through the pages; after a moment she quietly excused herself.

Saul watched her go, his hand flat over a particularly ingenious position.

Emma was surprised to find herself so quickly back in her own bedroom. She closed the door and locked it behind her.

A pillow book! Like a leather G-string from her Triple Zed lover. Again—to some people this was love?

Irene lay crumpled in a corner of the small room, the guitar meant for Saul lying between her and the small amplifier. The leads were all still plugged together, the power plug was still switched on. Emma took in the black face; the appearance of a witch had been made complete.

She hadn't touched Irene, she hadn't touched the guitar.

Now it seemed to Emma that the electric shock which had crumpled Irene had also given her some kind of secondary shock. How could she have left Irene like that, how could she have calmly replaced the fuse in the fusebox and completed a whole university assignment? Wasn't there something too that she had forgotten?

And why was it she only saw now that the photo pressed into her mirror was not of a person but of the past? She took the photo, folded it once, twice, dropped it into her wastepaper basket. Irene's black face demanded attention.

How was Emma to explain this to the authorities?

Finally a wave of horror and nausea swept over her, like a wave breaking over a tired swimmer. Here was black-faced Irene and just across the hall a bloated Saul was waiting in his bed—with that book at the ready. Emma passed her hands across her cheeks and was surprised when they felt as if they were full of fever. What had she forgotten?

She couldn't leave Irene just as she was. Before calling the police she would have to move her from that awful crumpled position in the corner. The guitar was between them.

Didn't they always say: touch nothing?

But Irene looked so pathetic. Emma shifted the amplifier out of the way and reached for the guitar. Even as she remembered that the wall plug was turned on and the house fuse was repaired and everything was still as live as it had been for Irene, Emma's hand went to the neck of the guitar.

Saul!

Emma's mind cried out for him as her forgetful fingers closed on the unearthed G-string, and there was a mild *Phut!* in the room.

Across the hallway, the lights went out in Saul's bedroom, filling him with expectation. Poor shy little Emma, but the drawn curtains let enough light in anyway. In a minute she would come through the door. The palms of his hands had become damp as he thumbed the glossy pages of his Japanese manual. Yes, in a minute little Emma would have what she wanted. Saul was excited, nervous, he was unsure how to carry himself with her. What would he say? He thought of all the years he had been her guardian and had watched her grow.

In this, he knew, there was no harm, only—as they had all known back in the sixties—love.

He tried to think of useful words to make her relax in his bed, but none came. In spite of his tenderness for Emma, he thought only to paraphrase the words of Bondo-san he had memorised so long ago in his early teenage years.

Just as Bondo-san had said to Kissy Suzuki, Saul would say fiercely, 'Emma, take off your clothes and lie down there. We'll start at page one.' And if this was her first and she was to cry out, her tears would be as insignificant as those of a sparrow.

ICE

Waiting in Prins Hendrik Park, Charlie Davis gazed across the frozen surface of the lake. He watched the many children, two adults and one handsome Belgian hound chase a soccer ball that seemed always just out of reach. Elsewhere on the lake teenagers rode bicycles in circles, a couple took off their gloves and held hands as they walked, joggers ran down from the banks onto the ice leaving their Reebok marks in the hard-packed snow. The brisk air carried the skidding of ice skates and the laughter of children as Charlie shivered on a wooden bench.

Mist hung like a pall over the lake. Beneath the mist a little girl with her hair in braids ran and fell, sliding on her backside into two smaller boys and knocking them over like a children's version of ten pin bowls. Then the hound was down with them and the echo of its bark seemed to crack across the vast frozen surface of the lake, called De Ijzeren Vrouw.

Charlie huddled in his Parisian overcoat and listened to the chattering of his teeth. Soon the cold had his eyes watering but he would not leave the bench, at least not for a bit longer—after all, if she did come he didn't want to miss her.

Two joggers in matching blue outfits were approaching on the running path which follows the lake all the way around its usually marshy banks, skirting the large indoor swimming and diving complex at the north-eastern reach. Now they were past him; Charlie envied their sweat and the mist which strained from their mouths and reminded him of how uncomfortably cold—freezing!—he was. The joggers had been going around and around De Ijzeren Vrouw as if they had no imagination for other places to run.

Charlie had been watching them for an hour, the exact time he had been early. Now it was just gone midday and he found himself staring expectantly toward the Muntelbolwerk, the most likely way she would arrive—if she came at all. There had been plenty of Belgian beer on New Year's Eve. Who could blame her if now on the second of January she had forgotten the vague arrangement they had made?

Charlie drew his feet up under the bench, mildly cursing the cold. So far he'd had everything this trip: the muggy humidity on leaving Sydney, the rain in Nice, the sleet at Heathrow, now snow in Holland. And before this holiday tacked onto the end of his trip, endless meetings attended with two tissue boxes stuffed into his pockets.

What a relief it had been to finally leave London and the parent company's executives. He had been invited to many end-of-year office parties in London and Putney, but there would have been all the couples, the music and champagne, and sooner or later someone would have asked about Helen and the boys. On impulse he had decided to miss them all and spend his Christmas break in the Netherlands, seeing out the decade in a town where he knew no one.

He remembered the seven-hour night ferry from Harwich to Den Haag, the cramped little cabin where he had slept a few hours, the bar on C Deck where he drank with a rowdy group of Scottish soldiers going on leave. A smile came to Charlie's face.

She was a quarter-hour late.

The skies were solemn and before late afternoon there would be more snow or rain—or both—but Charlie felt expectant and curiously free.

He looked from the Muntelbolwerk back to the lake. The children were calling out to each other, all of them rugged up against the cold. Most who were skating were really quite proficient. In contrast, Brian and Matthew would be in their little Batman bathers most of the holiday break, getting too much sun and slowly being poisoned by the foul waters of Sydney's beaches. Or maybe Helen would have splurged and taken the boys up to the Queensland beaches—a week at the new Noosa Sheraton, a few more days at the Coolum Hyatt.

It didn't matter where it was, the boys would be having fun. At eight and ten all they needed was the sand and the waves. Charlie imagined their reddening cheeks as they stood holding hands, ankle deep in the water and the froth of the breaking waves skimming towards them.

—This is ex! Matthew, the oldest would say.

—Really ex! little Brian would agree.

Charlie had one day listened around the Frenchs Forest head office to learn whether adults were using this popular new adjective—it seemed that for the time being it was only for the kids.

He stood up from the bench and stamped his feet, looking around, smiling. For him, *this* was ex.

The runners were back up toward the indoor swimming and diving centre. Behind him in a small animal enclosure that held rabbits and goats and winter birds, an animal started bleating with the sound of a drunkard's snores. Away on the ice the children started a singsong he couldn't understand.

Amongst all those on the ice there came a young man in a drab coat and beanie, pushing a bicycle. The figure crossed from the far corner of the lake, taking to the hard surface as a shortcut. Charlie couldn't see himself doing that, he was terrified by the frozen surface. The whole time he had been waiting he had heard the creaking and cracking of the ice shifting, settling, moving.

And that morning the caretaker's wife at his hotel had told him of a terrible winter four or five years back when two children and a dachshund had been lost through some thin ice at a corner of De Ijzeren Vrouw. He watched the children playing; there was no way he would have let Brian or Matthew onto that ice, no matter how safe it was supposed to be.

And she wasn't coming either—it had been too much to ask after all. Charlie stamped his feet again, took off his gloves and rubbed his palms together, then slowly pulled the gloves back on. His hair was wet and matted, and he wished he had a beanie like the one the young man walking his bicycle across the lake was wearing. One more look up to the Muntelbolwerk: only slow local traffic and a group of road workers in orange overalls.

There was a sharp cry from the ice. The little girl in braids and a yellow coat had fallen again, and this time the young man in the beanie was there to help her to her feet. The bicycle was lying on the hard snow covering the ice; as the young man bent for the little girl's hand the beanie fell away and long blonde-brown hair spilled out.

Charlie's smile broadened and he wondered if there was such a thing as spontaneous sex in a country of overcoats and scarves and thick woollen beanies. The blonde-brown hair on New Year's Eve had smelled of smoke and crowds—he imagined the fresh smell of snow and cold in it now.

The child hadn't hurt herself, her cry might only have been part of the game for when she rejoined her friends they were laughing and milling around her. Charlie watched Anika pick up her bicycle and brush snow from the pedals and gears. Her name was uppermost in his mind and he repeated it softly to himself—'Anika, Anika'—as if he was trying to put the name and face together.

He walked down the bank and felt the crunch of cold brittle grass under his boots. As she pushed her bicycle, her open overcoat flapping around her legs, Anika smiled up toward him. In his excitement Charlie nearly walked from the bank onto the surface of the lake, but he remembered the cracking sounds, the lost children and dachshund.

Anika's long hair seemed familiar to him, but he couldn't think from where. Now she was so close he could see the pink in her cheeks, the cheap palm-gloves that left her fingers exposed. On the handlebars of her bicycle, Anika's small fingers seemed bitter-red, raw with the cold.

Behind her, the group of children were singing.

There was no sun and little early light, but the sound of the baby crying woke Anika to the greyness of her flat. Through the skylight she saw the bleak sky of morning.

Molina's baby continued to cry in the flat downstairs; as usual, it would take Molina an hour to rouse herself and attend to the little girl. But the crying of the baby was anything but bad, it seemed a beautiful sound. As she lay huddled under the blankets Anika could imagine the child lying in the crib, her little face puckered with rage, the pink gums exposed and the firm tongue quivering with every cry. The bedclothes would be pushed away by the kicking feet, the small fists would be balled and shaking.

Anika saw herself holding Molina's baby, she could smell the baby smell and feel the hard gums tug at her breast. Under the blankets of her bed Anika was warm, but soon she remembered the ice and her hatred returned. Molina downstairs, Molina with her baby. Anika hugged herself tightly.

'Won't that brat ever shut up?' the indistinct voice spoke in English beside her. Anika drew a deep heavy breath and rolled toward him. Charlie was already asleep again. She spooned herself to his thin frame but with his face turned aside it was as impersonal as hugging the plaster cast of a man.

The skylight showed the cloudy January morning.

If only she could do what Molina had done, but beside the bed were the two empty packets. Anika sat up and stared at their labels. A yellow pencil drawing of a bee pollinating a flower, the word *vrijkaartje*—free ticket—on each in big letters. The nightclubs and bars had been handing these out with the price of admission since 1986.

The baby Ilke's cries were softer now, through the thin and cracked plaster walls you heard everything. Anika stood from the bed and slipped on a housecoat, turned up the gas fire and started making coffee. Ilke downstairs, so close she could have been a part of her. The lack of privacy; Anika thought she could even place the long night that Ilke was conceived, Molina drunk and with her own *vrijkaartjes* forgotten in a dresser drawer. The father, who was the father? But that was hardly the point.

The point was Ilke crying in the crib while Molina snored. Anika remembered the ice and shivered even though the room was now very warm. She left the coffee to brew and went downstairs to nurse Ilke and shake Molina awake.

When she returned to the two rooms that made up her rent-subsidised flat, the air was heavy with the aroma of fresh coffee. The gas heater had gone too high and the flames behind the glass gave off too much radiant heat for the small open area that was her kitchen and bedroom and dining room. Anika poured herself a cup of black coffee and arranged a hard-backed chair so that she could sit facing the bed while also looking out her window at the grimy Vughterstraat below. The old buildings across the way showed no lights this grey morning.

It could have been Wym sleeping in the bed, Charlie Davis under the covers was such a shapeless bundle. But it was short black hair on the pillow, not Wym's long red hair. So many years, Anika told herself, but her memory was more vivid with each passing year, almost in inverse proportion to what she really wanted. When they had first found the flat it had seemed perfect; now the new Moroccan landlord only ever came for the rent and refused to attend to the building's old pipes.

The woman Molina in the downstairs flat with a child and a small dog had seemed perfect too all those years ago, and for a time—

In the bed, Charlie Davis yawned and turned. He'd told her about his career as a businessman, how he was the managing director of a British company in Australia. It was like having a government minister in her bed—the minister for international relations and *vrijkaartjes*.

He was waking slowly, which was unsurprising. After their meeting by the lake Charlie had taken her to lunch in an expensive place she had only ever ridden her bicycle by, and that lunch had become a long evening's conversation over a bottle of

Bols gin. When he was sitting up she poured him some coffee.

'Just black thanks.' His hair was tousled and he was smiling at her. Anika had forgotten all the necessary words, especially in English. She wanted to ask him what he wanted for breakfast, did he want a shower, was any of this at all important to him.

But she was glad when he took her by the wrist and the coffee was left on the bedside table to grow cold. She laughed when he cried out at the third little packet with the bee pollinating the flower on it, then when he was over her he was laughing too:

'This is ex!'

'This is sex?' Anika asked, unable to comprehend.

Later she made toast and they sat in bed with more coffee. Charlie was watching the framed print that hung on the opposite wall.

'She's my favourite,' he said, and Anika turned to his profile. His nose was thin and long but there was a strong chin under his few days' stubble. She liked to watch his lips when he spoke for she thought them as full as a harlot's. 'The Lady of Shalott, painted by Waterhouse in 1888. The original is in the Tate Gallery in London.'

'She is very beautiful.' Anika wanted her English to be precise, to sound right. She found that she wanted everything to be right for him. 'And sad.'

'I don't know.' The coarse grain of his beard was against her cheek. 'When you were walking across the lake and I was watching your hair, I knew it reminded me of something.' His hands touched her hair, gently ran through it and spread it like a shawl over her bare shoulders. 'Or someone. Now I know,' he said, and they both stared at her in the print, the long golden-brown hair with the band in it, the earnest expression as she sat forward in the bow of the little boat.

'Outside the isle a shallow boat
Beneath a willow lay afloat
Below the cavern stern she wrote—'

'The Lady of Shalott,' Anika finished the stanza for him. 'Do you know all of it?'

'Most of it, especially when I've had a few.'

Anika took his face in her hands and kissed Charlie as she might have kissed Wym in the best of their days. Businessman/whiskyman, quoting from Tennyson, too old for someone as young as her. She kissed him for the way he was with her and the nice things he said to her; she kissed him too for not asking about the framed photo of the little boy that hung beside the Lady of Shalott.

The Uilenburg family hotel where he was staying was small and quiet, but each of the four guest rooms was more spacious than anything a Sheraton or Hilton could offer. There was heavy furniture and dark wood panelling on the walls, the bed could easily have accommodated four people. A large bedside table carried a plate of mints, a bottle of Evian water, a bowl of fruit.

It was several days later and Charlie woke alone to his spacious surroundings. From the distant door there came the polite tapping of Mrs Uilenburg bringing his breakfast tray.

He strode barefoot across the Turkish rugs, enjoying again the comfort of the hotel. The past days had been spent at Anika's. He didn't mind her small flat but the constantly crying baby downstairs had finally driven him out for at least one morning of sleeping in late. It was now well past nine—luxury!

He thanked Mrs Uilenburg and took his tray to the dining table in the centre of the room. There was a yellow tulip in a vase, a pot of tea, orange juice, warm toast wrapped in linen napkins. When he switched on the classical music station a piece from the Brandenburg Concertos was playing. God, why not hole up here in s'Hertogenbosch for a month? Through the lace curtains he saw that the weather had not improved. There were heavy clouds and snow; in the mirror he admired the way his beard was coming along.

He was thinking of Anika and the bars they went to in the

evenings, he was thinking what it was like to stay in bed late
and have breakfast to the music of Bach. Back home it would
be thirty-eight degrees and the boys would be crying because
their skin was peeling from too much sun, Helen would be in a
temper trying to keep them away from the beaches.

Too much business, too much marriage; in this place where
he was a stranger he was as free as he'd been when he was a
teenager. Charlie poured himself some tea and finished off the
marmalade with a bit of toast. He'd wanted to be away from
Anika for a night, to wake up alone and gloat.

But now that was done and he already wanted to see her.

Mrs Uilenburg or one of the spotty Uilenburg daughters had
laundered his dirty clothes and pressed his shirts for him. After
a hot shower he dressed quickly, then took his time with the
final layers. A sweater, a scarf tied the way Anika had showed
him for the most warmth, gloves, a beanie she had bought him
in the local Vroom & Dreisman store, the Parisian overcoat bun-
dling it all together. As he left the vast room and bumped his
way down the dark corridor he felt as awkward as an astronaut.

Outside in the wind and snow, however, everyone was
dressed the same way and he felt perfectly at home. For such
an awful day there were many people about. Instead of heading
straight to Anika's flat he let himself follow the others to the
town square. There was slush and black ice in the gutters, people hurried to get out of the cold, the smell of frying fish was in
the air. In the large flat square around the statue of Hieronymus
Bosch, the stalls were set up. Market day.

The snow came in dribs and drabs, melting as it hit the
ground. Charlie went around the market square amongst the
crowded anonymity of coats and caps. Men and women carried
shopping bags, bicycles were tethered in racks by the roadside.
Once he thought he saw Anika standing by some cases of oranges, but the flash of long hair was quickly gone and the crowd
seemed more anonymous than before. He was getting to know
the vegetables and fruits: oranges and mandarins from Spain

or Portugal, spinach and leeks from Belgium, peaches and apricots from southern Italy. Tulips and other flowers lay in deep baskets everywhere. A floral scent was in the air, mingling with the smell of frying fish and potatoes which came from the little shops around the square. Charlie could feel himself responding; it was time to see Anika.

He crossed quiet cobbled streets until he was following laneways closed to all traffic other than bicycles and mopeds. Coffee shops along the way were either packed or occupied by only one or two sullen-faced Moroccans. Charlie thought of buying something for Anika in the large bookstore he came to—perhaps the collected works of Tennyson translated (and ruined) into Dutch—but he kept on through the slush as the snow turned to rain and the cold wind whipped at the rubbish left in these back laneways.

As he turned a corner, a woman coming the other way bumped into him and kept going. He saw only a wisp of hair under a tightly knotted scarf, a grey coat that gave nothing away. But he smelled fresh perfume and, when he turned to watch, the strong wind made her keep her skirts down with her hands. Charlie was glad Anika was so close.

In the Vughterstraat, he stood across from the small tottering building where she lived. He looked toward her second floor window but there was no light. The place had once been a house, the middle class family home of a merchant or banker, and there were many others like it in the long street. Not all had become flats. A little further down there was a sex shop, peep show, a cheese delicatessen and a macrobiotic society's grocery store.

Charlie put his hands into his pockets for they had become quite numb. It bothered him that there was no light in Anika's window. He needed her to be home. A few doors down the sex shop's garish neon sign came alive.

The old building had good heating. When he finally crossed the street and pushed open the front door, the sudden warmth was overpowering. Shutting the door behind him to keep out the wind, he struggled out of his coat and outer layers, hanging them on a peg along the hallway wall.

The flat of the woman with the baby was down here, Anika's was upstairs.

As if trained to be a sentinel against intruders, the baby started to howl as he quietly walked to the staircase. His cheeks were flushed with the warmth; he needed to take off his shirt and singlet.

'She is not home this morning,' a voice behind him said, and in the semi-darkness he felt as if he had been caught doing something covert. It was the woman, standing in her front doorway, holding the baby and nursing it to keep it quiet. Anika had introduced them one afternoon but he had forgotten the names.

'My name is Molina,' she said to remind him. 'This is Ilke.' The woman's features were strong and dark, her wide eyes were amused.

'I remember,' Charlie smiled though he felt an unusual awkwardness. Had Molina been watching him from behind her curtain as he stared at Anika's window and the sex shop facade? The baby's chin was awash with dribble. 'Do you know when Anika will be back?'

'It is Saturday. Anika does her marketing on Saturday. Before Ilke I used to do it with her every Saturday. Now she brings groceries for me also. But first she will go to the cathedral to see De Lieve Vrouw. Every Saturday it is the same.' Molina started to smile and Charlie liked the lines at the corners of her mouth. 'Anika prefers to be on schedule.'

He wanted to ask her about what she had said—De Lieve Vrouw—for he had no idea what Molina was referring to. The baby dribbled from its chin to its bib, which seemed stained with egg yolk or some other sort of baby food. Charlie took in Molina's strong dark features as she dabbed at Ilke's face with a tissue. Molina might have been partly of Surinam origin; he remembered a little of the history. Holland surrendering the American town of New Amsterdam to the Duke of York in exchange for the country of Surinam. Seventeenth century? He couldn't remember, it had been just another foundation stone in the old colonial empire.

'You will wait for Anika? There will be more snow.'

'How long do you think she'll be?'

'One hour or two hours. I have coffee.'

He wasn't given the chance to refuse and he wasn't sure that he would have. As she turned and led him into her flat, Ilke looked back at him from over Molina's shoulder. The baby's eyes were perfectly round and green, the skin was milky and there were bright spots of pink in the cheeks, as if they had been painted there. He made a face at Ilke; the child creased its soft brow.

'You will sit here,' Molina said, and pushed a hard wooden chair toward Charlie. The flat was the double of the one on the upper floor. She poured coffee from the pot which was simmering on the gas stove. 'You will have a shortbread.'

He liked the imperative in the way she spoke English. 'I will have a shortbread,' he replied in a similar tone, and Molina looked up and laughed with him. 'Where did you learn to speak English?' he asked, wanting to add—from a drill sergeant?

'The cinema and the television. Where I went to school they did not offer languages. But all the young girls wish to speak English.'

Charlie thought Molina was probably a little older than she looked. Her hands seemed as if they had seen hard work and when she laughed the lines around her eyes deepened. In her flat it was even warmer than it had been in the hallway outside. She was wearing only a thin wraparound skirt and a halter top that showed off her smooth round shoulders and dark skin.

On a side-table there was Bols gin in a ceramic bottle, but Molina took a bottle of whisky and added some to each cup of coffee. As she did she looked at Charlie; the warmth of the flat

seemed ready to overpower him, then he was saying, 'I see you
have one too.' He indicated the framed print hanging on the
wall above the baby's crib. Beside it there was a photograph of a
small boy, just as in Anika's flat. He studied the young face and
wasn't sure if it was the same child or not.

'A present from Anika. For strength, this is why she gives it to
me. You like her?'

'Oh sure, it's one of my favourites. Waterhouse painted it in
1888. The original's hanging—'

Molina made a face. 'I do not like it but I do not want to of-
fend Anika. She needs strength.' Molina made a gesture with
her hand that said—but I do not. 'She wishes that I would go
with her to the St Jin's Cathedral to see De Lieve Vrouw too. She
would like me to pray with her.' She smiled at Charlie, a full
and radiant smile that took him by surprise. It was so warm in
the flat he wanted to run his finger around his tight collar. 'But
I have Ilke.'

She turned her smile to the baby in its crib. Ilke was asleep
now, and they listened to the soft sounds she made.

'Anika chooses not to forget,' Molina said to Charlie, as if he
understood.

'Those words in Dutch you said, the second time now. I'm
sorry but I don't understand.'

'De Lieve Vrouw? Then you do not know Anika well.' Her
smile toward him had an unsettling edge. The whisky in the
coffee made it hard for him to catch his breath, he could feel
the sweat in his armpits and on his brow. Through the window
he saw that Molina had been correct. The drizzle was now snow
and he could hear the whistling of the wind. 'In English it means
"The Sweet Lady". But not like her,' she went on, indicating the
Lady of Shalott. 'The Sweet Lady is our local heroine. A statue
of the Virgin Mother that stands in her own tiny chapel of St
Jin's Cathedral. Everyone knows her.'

In the way Molina spoke there was something as unsettling
as her smile.

'She make miracles for we poor Dutch, so people go and pray to her or sit with her to pass the time. She has a legend.'

Charlie toyed with the handle of his coffee cup, wondering if she was teasing him. 'Yes?'

'There was a terrible battle many centuries ago and a cathedral here in s'Hertogenbosch was completely destroyed. The statue of the Virgin was lost in the fire, forever it seemed. But twenty-five years ago some workmen found her buried in the mud of one of the canals just near the town centre. The statue, they say, was as perfect as it had been so long ago and she was restored to her proper place. St Jin's was built where the first cathedral had been. Ever since she makes miracles for lost souls.' Molina smiled at him. 'Is there a nice story like this where you come from?'

'Maybe one or two, I'm not sure that I'd know.'

Their cups were empty and Molina poured more coffee, more whisky. Charlie wanted to escape; the smooth line of her cheek when she looked toward the crib made him want to stay.

'They say there are miracles, Charlie,' she went on, using his name for the first time. He liked the way she emphasised both syllables. 'There is an old statue in a cathedral. I have other things to do.' Again she smiled toward Ilke and he found he wanted to touch the deep lines around her eyes. 'But Anika is a great admirer of strong women.'

She stood from the table to check on Ilke in the crib. Charlie watched her. He hadn't before noticed that she was barefoot. Molina looked small and strong in her halter and cheap skirt, the clothes so incongruous with the snow outside. But the warmth of the flat made him undo the top button of his collar and wipe away the perspiration on his face. Molina was smoothing Ilke's blanket; his eyes were drawn to her bare arms and shoulders.

'Who is that boy in the photo?' he asked. Many times in Anika's flat he had wanted to ask the same question but something had held him back. With Molina it was different.

She touched her palm to her sleeping child's cheek. 'The same as with Anika.'

'It's the same little boy?' he said, not understanding.

Molina paused, then walked to the table where he sat. She stood facing him and he thought she seemed as compact and strong as a dancer. 'No, Charlie. That is my little boy. The photo in Anika's room is of her own.' Her lips seemed to tremble and Charlie again felt the need to touch the skin around Molina's eyes.

It happened so slowly that it was like a dream; she continued to look straight at him and let him see her tears.

The whisky in the second cup of coffee, the warmth of the room, the perspiration on his face. Slowly-slowly he understood. He wanted to say,

—Is that your son, Molina, did he die with Anika's little boy? Did you replace your boy with a tiny baby while your friend upstairs prays to a statue for a miracle?

His eyes moved to the Lady of Shalott and the face was Anika's.

Molina sat at the table on a chair beside him and finished her coffee. Charlie watched her hand resting on the cheap laminex tabletop and could not imagine wanting a woman more. As the baby started to softly snore and the snow came down outside, he covered Molina's hand with his own.

Anika looked up sharply.

Her shopping bag had tilted from where it had been standing on the marble floor by her knees. An orange and some pears had rolled across the ground toward three fat old ladies sitting further up the pew. They watched her with distaste, as if a drunkard or an addict had wandered into the holy chapel, but a thin man of about seventy put out a trembling hand for the orange and gave it back to her. Anika thanked him as quietly as she could and recovered the pears. When she raised herself from her knees and sat back on the hard wooden pew she felt the old man's eyes still upon her.

There was a smile from the bloodless lips before the hands came together and the old man bowed his head to his prayers once more. Every part of him was shaking with his disease, and Anika looked up, not at De Lieve Vrouw, but at the walls of the chapel. They were covered in silver mementos of thanks: a small silver leg, a little pair of lungs, the heart of a child. A hundred of them, two hundred perhaps, symbols of all the parts of the body upon which the Virgin of plaster and stone had performed a miracle. Perhaps there were hundreds more in the cloisters of the great cathedral—the little chapel could only hold so many, after all.

And if there should be a miracle for her, what silver memento of thanks could she give for the thing she desired most?

The small blue eyes of the statue gazed at the front rows. The Mother of God to those who believed, but Anika quickly gathered up her shopping bag and neatly folded coat. The reverie had been too clear that morning, the projection from an eye that remembered every detail.

Anika had been on the frozen lake, Molina up ahead playing rough-house with her latest boyfriend, this one a Greek of no more than eighteen or nineteen.

'Take our photographs here,' Molina always laughing had called out, throwing the instamatic to her across metres of ice. Not surprisingly Anika dropped it, but the layer of fresh snow cushioned the fall. Molina had posed this way and that way with the Greek while Anika obediently snapped the photo.

Four years ago now, Anika thought as she left the chapel and pulled her scarf over her mouth. Four years and one month; she made sure she always knew.

It was surprising to have snow so early in the year, it was surprising too that De Ijzeren Vrouw was already frozen over. It had been like that four years and one month ago, everyone had loved the early ice. De Ijzeren Vrouw—the Iron Lady—so named because it wasn't a natural lake, but one made by heavy earthmoving equipment. Why were there so many women in her life? The Iron Lady, the Sweet Lady, the Lady of Shalott—and Molina.

Anika swapped the heavy shopping bag from one hand to the other. She was walking to the lake.

So long ago, Wym had had a cold. Smoking since the age of twelve had given him a poor chest. That day taking little Michael out so Wym could have some peace, meeting Molina downstairs with her new Greek, Molina's little Raphael rugged up against the cold and the stupid dachshund excited about going out and already trying to mount Michael's leg. Raphael and Michael holding hands and singing,

—De Ijzeren Vrouw, De Ijzeren Vrouw!

And then they were on the ice, Molina showing off with her boyfriend and the children running and sliding on the fresh fall of snow, the dog chasing them on its short legs.

Anika now stood at the side of the lake next to the bench where Charlie Davis had been waiting for her the day after New Year. As if it were happening again, she could see Molina through the instamatic's shutter, she could see the young Greek's eyes as wide as saucers, not believing his luck at such a beautiful woman pushing her chest into his arm. The boys were off running in their Alaskan coats and earmuffs, their squeals of delight and the barking of the dachshund all part of the fun. Back in the flat with a runny nose and a packet of unfiltered Camels, Wym had been keen to watch an Italian soccer game on the Sky channel.

Four years and one month.

After the hushed quiet of the chapel in St Jin's, the lake was like a festival playground. Anika took her heavy shopping bag and walked over the ice. Young people were riding bicycles in circles, here a group of tiny children were playing a game with a yellow ball, there older teenagers tried to impress each other with their ice-skating skills. At a far corner of the lake a hot food stall was set up and a tinny speaker on its roof gave out *The Skaters' Waltz.*

It was a dizzying world of falling snow and music. Anika wished she could go to them all, that she could run with the children and kick the yellow ball, that she could put on some ice skates and show the teenagers how she could still do a perfect figure eight.

It was Molina's fault, stupid sluttish Molina. Wanting her photo taken while the children had kept running toward the distant bank and the dog's barking had echoed into the trees. No one in s'Hertogenbosch had ever been warned of thin ice.

But Molina now had a new baby—where had she found the courage for such a thing?

So Anika stayed in the same building year after year and in the morning she went down and comforted little Ilke while Molina snored on. To understand and to stop hating Molina, for these things she asked De Lieve Vrouw.

Anika turned her face up to the snow and let it fall on her cold cheeks. Somehow it reminded her of Charlie. Charlie with his stubble and his stanzas from Tennyson.

It was past midday. She put the heavy shopping bag down for a moment then picked it up in her other hand. Perhaps he would be at the flat waiting for her. Hadn't he said her hair was like the Lady of Shalott's, hadn't he said he would take her to the Tate Gallery in London to see the original painting?

She felt like crying out and hugging herself. The laughter of those on the ice carried to her and she wanted to laugh with them. In her shopping bag there was spinach and leek and fresh fetta cheese, also too the most expensive bottle of red wine she had ever purchased. Tonight she would make a wonderful meal just for the two of them, she would touch the beard he was growing and look to see what was in his heart. And when she trusted him she would trust herself; as Molina had done, the *vrijkaartjes* would stay in her dresser drawer.

Anika checked her watch. It was late and she should be getting back to the flat to meet Charlie. Before she went she looked down at the hard ice between her feet. The local newspaper was already saying that in a week or two the ice would be melting.

NOW THAT THE WALL IS GONE

Now that the wall is gone, anyone who ever had a half-day visitor's pass into East Berlin has a personal story about the divided city.

This story, however, takes place in Switzerland and begins not with the Wall or with Checkpoint Charlie or with the guard posts set behind barbed wire, but with the hands of Katherine Spiegler. I remember that they were long and faultless hands; full of grace we Catholics might have said. Well preserved, her doctor or gigolo might have thought.

It was my friend Helmut who first introduced me to Katherine Spiegler. Helmut and I were travelling together through Europe in late 1986, and when we ran out of money we ran to his distant relatives in Lausanne. We were in time for a family wedding, and at the reception I found myself seated next to an elegant old lady in white—the embodiment of Mary spending her winter years with St John in the Anatolian city of Ephesus.

Helmut had liked to tell me about his Aunt Katherine and her associate, Werner—fortyish, correct, dead-eyed—and about her photographs, which in those years you could have found in almost any glossy European magazine, and her escape from East Berlin in 1969. Through the Wall, as they say, where Captain Spiegler was killed, dying a defector against the border patrol's gunfire while a younger Frau Spiegler was dragged on into the West. Helmut had warned me not to bring these things up with her—as if I would have.

The reception took place in a lounge overlooking the dark waters of Lake Geneva. Helmut's family are German-Swiss so most of the conversations took place in their language. But his Aunt Katherine was happy to speak English with me, which she did throughout the bombastic speeches. Of course it was her hands that I first noticed, then her delicate frame all long and slender in the white lace dress. I was surprised when she invited me to visit the next day.

'Please be punctual at midday,' she had said. 'Werner likes to serve our drinks exactly at twelve on Sunday.'

So the next day I made certain to be on time. Katherine Spiegler greeted me under the broad arch of her drawing room's entrance as a tall dark clock in the corridor echoed midday throughout the great house. My eyes went to her perfect hands, which I could have pressed to my lips. Instead we shook hands in the firm German tradition Helmut's family had long since made me used to.

Werner was punctual too.

He presented us with a champagne cocktail each, not exactly what I'd been expecting for Sunday's midday drinks. They came on a silver tray with ornate edges and though I'd met Werner at the wedding, he didn't speak to me. A curt bow under the mahogany arch of the huge room was his exit line.

The cocktails sat politely before us on a low table as I listened to Katherine Spiegler talk about her work.

'But there is a certain image that is more difficult to deal with. The immediately recognisable, so to speak, but with the many levels evident. Such as the icons we use for our modern culture. The Christ figure, the hammer and sickle, the black baby at a puckered nipple. These are simple images but they perfectly convey their complexity, their many layers. Yes? And to find new images as these'—she shrugged, looking down to her flute glass as if that might have presented yet another lost image—'is the challenge. I detest the obscure. Equally well I detest the simple-minded, what you would call the clear definition of black and white. The difference I believe is there, the difference between nice photography and great images.'

'I understand,' I said to be polite, and she nodded at me with satisfaction. It was only in the silence that followed that I realised she was waiting for me to continue. 'The Christ figure is interesting,' I went on, searching a little desperately, 'the many images that invokes in people's minds whether they're the faithful or not. Similarly other things. The pyramids, the peace sign from the sixties.' I felt panicky at how quickly I was running out of ideas. But there was the obvious one after all and before I could stop myself the words came out. 'The Berlin Wall.'

A quiet smile came to Katherine's lips and as I watched her I saw that the skin of her face and neck was as flawless as that of her hands. Was she in her seventies? During the wedding reception the previous evening Katherine Spiegler in white had resembled an icon herself—the Mother of Christ.

The sun seemed to have lowered even though it wasn't much past midday. A yellow light shone against our profiles. And I'd mentioned the Wall. There was quiet as she continued to smile. Neither of us touched our drinks.

As if he had been listening at the door for the appropriate time to enter, Werner appeared under the arch again. This time he was carrying a tripod and a camera. At his feet was a large rectangular metal box that must have held other photographic equipment. It seemed he was ready to prepare Katherine Spiegler for work. He gently put the tripod and camera down then held a light meter up in front of his eyes, checking readings here and there.

'Not now, Werner,' she said sharply. 'Upstairs, take it upstairs won't you?' The English was for my benefit and I saw the muscle in Werner's jaw become a knot. He abruptly dropped the light meter and it swung from his neck like an ugly necklace. 'And bring us our coats.' Katherine rose to her feet in a manner that made me think the visit was over. Instead she said, 'You have only been in Lausanne a week?'

'A couple of days actually. Next week, after we've hitched to Vevey and Montreux, we'll take the night train over to Barcelona.'

'You must make an effort to see more of Lausanne before

you go. Do not let the weather deter you. In our terms, this is the mildest of winters. Still, you will need your coat and scarf.' She turned then, and in the yellow light that filtered through the windows she lost twenty, thirty years. 'If you will take an afternoon stroll with me?'

And Werner was back, waiting beneath the wooden arch with my coat and scarf over one arm, another set draped over the other. The light meter was still around his neck. I must admit I felt a moment of disappointment that he was to walk with us, but after Werner had us ready for the mild Swiss winter he walked off. His heels clickety-clacked as he disappeared and the memory of his wet-lipped smile was all that remained.

As we left I thought I saw the blue split-second light of a camera's flash coming from somewhere deeper in the house.

'Is he taking photos?'

Katherine Spiegler's smile could have meant anything.

Outside the great house she shared with Werner—'We all bet he's her lover, but nobody will ask her!'—it was as cold as anything I'd ever experienced. It was somewhere below five degrees but the weather didn't seem to bother her. We walked through a back garden that was in desperate need of care, then through a rusted gate in a wire fence. The house, like the lounge where the wedding reception was held, overlooked the great lake and soon we were arm in arm, nestled against each other like the oldest of friends, strolling along the clean esplanade that follows the Lausanne reaches of Lake Geneva.

'It is your art that allows you the time to travel so?' she asked as if I was some kind of wealthy painter. There was of course a hint of humour in her voice.

'And the restaurant work. I'm lucky that the past few Christmas breaks I've had the time to come to Europe. And pay for it the rest of the year, I'm afraid.'

'But it is your art that funds you.'

It was easy to laugh when she was so obviously teasing me, and with her arm so warm in mine I couldn't help but wonder at the twenty or thirty year age difference between her and Werner.

'I paint landscapes in water colour. It's hardly what you would call art.'

But she was already changing the subject; my water colours were as dull to her as they were to me.

'You have been to Germany? Berlin?' The sound of her voice was different again, an old woman's voice, and the lake seemed overcome with winter cold. I remembered her in the drawing room with the low sunlight against her profile and I thought,— *Yes, this had to come.*

'The year before last. Just a few days.'

'West Berlin. And the crossing to the East? It is very easy for a tourist, yes?' Katherine drew my arm closely to her as if I'd shown some sign of the cold. There was sharp colour around her high cheekbones. 'Did you hate East Berlin?'

'Well ...' but I was unsure what to say. 'It was only an after-noon, not even a whole day. The place I guess is pretty easy to—dislike. But it's fascinating in its own way.'

'Please. Do not feel you must be guarded. It has been so long since I was there. Twenty years and more, but things change only slightly. West Berlin thrives with its industry and wealth, a special kind of ugliness. I have photographed whole streets where the cars are Porsche, Mercedes Benz, BMW, over and over, end to end. And East Berlin dies in its industry—perfect ugliness. Fallen buildings, dirt and crude oil in the gutters. And the Wall as you so correctly spoke, the perfect image of our century.'

I didn't look at Katherine Spiegler, I didn't want to see the edges of some old madness in her green eyes. Helmut had warned me of this. I watched instead the surface of the lake, the ducks skittering across the mist, the few boats moored and those further out, returning from the horizon.

'Did you feel it a pitiless place?'

'Well, no—'

'But art and thoughts and ideas, driven by none other than the State.'

I remembered something from that afternoon spent wandering around East Berlin, something that I thought would appease her. 'I saw soldiers goosestepping in a line. It was at a changing of the guard of some museum. The way they marched with their stiff arms and legs going up and down in unison, it was as if there had never been a war.'

She stopped a moment, kissed my cheek with lips that seemed unnaturally warm, took my arm so that we again walked as one, our pace faster now. 'Good, good, yes. Marching as if there had never been a war. It is just so.' Katherine Spiegler smiled at me in a way that made me feel a sudden inspiration had come over her. 'Let us return to the house. It is too cold this afternoon.' And in a moment we were striding back the way we had come and she was saying, 'Yes, I see why you are Helmut's good friend. Let me look at your eyes, yes, they are good eyes. Yes.'

Helmut, can you believe that I almost thought I was falling in love with your poor crazy aunt?

We walked back to the house and hung our coats and scarves on wall hooks in the vestibule. I thought that Werner would have appeared but he must have been otherwise occupied.

'Would you mind,' Katherine Spiegler asked me, 'would you mind posing as a subject for me? Your friendship with my nephew Helmut is important. I would like to capture this, and your eyes, of course.'

'When?' I hesitantly asked.

'Now! Now of course—you will come upstairs?'

I didn't know what to say or what to expect. 'I must go soon,' I said a little too quickly. 'Helmut's meeting me.'

'Good! That is perfect.'

And I was already following her up the staircase to the second floor, where the house was darker. There were few windows and the long quiet corridor gave on to many rooms whose

doors were shut. A musty odour was in the air. My companion
moved briskly, with authority. As I've said, it seemed that some
inspiration had come to her.

Katherine opened a door to reveal a huge room stuffed with
furniture and all kinds of paraphernalia. In the middle of the
room Werner was struggling with his camera tripod and lights.
Katherine spoke to him in German. In answer, he smiled his
wet-lipped smile at me.

I walked amongst the cupboards and chests of the room.
The dark walls were covered with framed photographs and
heavy purple curtains covered the windows, but what drew my
attention were the many costumes hanging in the open closets.

'Yes, look at them, that is right. We once had a magic shop in
Lausanne, but there was more business in providing costumes
for children's parties. Now I sometimes use them for this,' she
said, indicating the expensive camera. Looming in a corner was
a huge stuffed bear. 'Look at him, his name is Hans. The children loved him!'

I looked from the bear to Werner, who was putting silver
reflective shades up to the dismountable lights. How had he
known Katherine Spiegler wanted to photograph me?

But she was running her wonderful hands over the shoulders of the hanging garments. 'Take off your coat and try this
one, perhaps it will suit you.' She moved a mirror-stand for me
so that as I slipped on a bandleader's gold and red braided jacket I could see myself better. 'And this,' she laughed, crowning
me with a top hat which was also gold and red but which was
much too large. In the mirror I saw my dark eyes staring out
from under the brim. I remember thinking then how unsettled
I looked.

Katherine Spiegler turned for something else and I saw another pair of dark eyes, from a framed photograph on the wall.
The photograph was of an army officer with a stern face and
moustache. It was centred amongst all the others and was a great
deal larger. While I stood in my outfit the serious young officer

looked on; I quickly took off the ridiculous jacket and hat.

Werner was straightening from setting up the lights and now rubbed his hands together briskly. He was smiling.

'Find the Pentax, I will take a few snaps with that to start,' Katherine said in English, then from a deep drawer took a brown parcel tied with string. She placed it on top of a glass display case. Her slender fingers struggled with the knots.

'Can I help?'

'Please do not touch.'

From out of the brown paper she unwrapped a clean grey coat, an army jacket of sorts. There were no braids or symbols, no markings of rank, only plain stitched seams and black buttons which spoke of war as plainly as the gunfire of a distant battle. Katherine held it out for me. Her face was intent and her lips were parted. I slipped on the jacket, standing again before the mirror.

'Do up the buttons,' she said, and as I did my fingers were drawn to three neatly resewn holes in the left side, beneath the ribs. In the strangeness of the room Katherine Spiegler's smile seemed anything but happy. 'Yes, I believe here is the image.'

Werner returned to the room. He was fitting a flash into the Pentax when he saw me wearing the jacket. An expression of sadness came to his face. The strength seemed to go from him.

'Oh Katherina, *nein*.'

She ignored him, taking the Pentax from his weak hands. 'You will allow me to photograph you like this? Here we could have very strong magic, do you not think, Werner—if we wished it so?'

Werner didn't say a word.

And Katherine Spiegler herself seemed to hesitate. It was as if she was torn between the desire to take the photos and the desire to touch the jacket again. Finally it was too much; she passed the camera back to Werner. The palms of her soft hands reached out to press against the resewn holes of the jacket. From the wall, Captain Spiegler's dark eyes watched us.

I could feel her palms as they pressed warmly to my ribs. Her face was so close I could have kissed her.

She hates the obscure, I told myself, the black and white. Here she has found the magic—Katherine Spiegler's new interpretation of the Berlin Wall. But this, her own depiction of the many layers, was somehow too perfect; through the jacket I could feel her graceful hands trembling.

I remember that we stayed in the strange room of the great house the whole afternoon. Now of course there is no need to establish such images. On every late evening news broadcast you can see souvenir hunters chipping away at what is left of the Wall. You can buy your own little piece of icon from the black market, you can even get it by mail order—now that the Wall is gone.

JUMPING AT THE MOON

Veronica and Benson live in Annandale, in a Federation house Veronica inherited when her septuagenarian grandmother met a rich widower named Harry and went to live with him in North Queensland.

Benson came with the house.

It's a quiet house with a long sunny corridor, and bedrooms I've never seen. It's the type of house you can remember from your childhood. Wooden pegs, galvanised iron roof, a linoleum floor in the kitchen. Wartime porcelain and crockery behind the patterned glass of a mahogany display cabinet. It's that part of our country that only lives in memories. But there are a lot of memories in that house too; some of them are Veronica's, some may even belong to Benson. In his new condition I'm told he spends a great deal of time sleeping the sleep of the innocent, the outraged, the newly neutered.

None of the memories are mine of course.

On cold nights during a full moon, Veronica might sit outside on her broad verandah in one of the rickety wooden chairs her grandfather used to restore. Benson might come and jump into her lap, and the two of them might watch the pale moon through the branches and leaves of the old tree that grows in front of the house. It's a quiet street and the only sound would be the cool breeze rustling the leaves, car headlights the only real movement, moving white and slow across the face of the house. Inside, the beds would be empty and the fire would be out.

Veronica and Benson might look at that moon and feel some sense of the connection between them. Or they might just be thinking about vampire movies.

I've been in Veronica and Benson's house four or five times. Four times. I've held Benson on my lap and rubbed his back, I've let him put his whiskers up to my face, I've let him dribble onto my knee. All of these things I would have preferred Veronica to be doing, even the dribbling—though she's a third the age of Benson.

When I was in hospital and recovering, they kept me pretty well anaesthetised all of the time.

I know there were lots of nurses, all of them pretty—at least in my mind. I could be as liberal in my mental interpretation of the nurses as I wanted to be. I was too far away to know what they looked like for sure. Voluptuous and willing, passionate and willing, erotic and willing, these were my angels.

I can't remember a face, I can't remember a voice, not of anyone in this world. Yet in my drugged, drifting state there was a friend, someone who lives on the other side of consciousness and who was there for me. I knew then and I know now that he was a total construction of my anaesthesia. I even know what memory I dreamed him up from. An old friend, Henk Wolkers, spent a lot of time in Holland experimenting with heroin. That was way back in the mid-seventies.

I used to be enthralled by his stories.

He went through a phase where he would hold the powdered drug between two knives and super heat it over a gas flame in order to inhale the fumes. On his trips into the nether world he discovered a spirit guide, a friend who'd experienced all of life's rich pageant—and it was all embossed into a huge tapestry that could have been life itself.

Henk was always a bit of some other world.

Once, in his many earthly travels, a tribe of Sioux Indians Henk befriended made him an honorary brave and gave him the name Speaking Spirit. Even the old Sioux tribesmen must have found Henk a little esoteric.

But that's another story.

So, with every heroin trip, Henk's new spirit friend would

tease him by lifting a corner of that tapestry and letting him catch a glimpse of—what? Henk said it was eternity, the starry blackness after life, the universe, the great collective soul, you name it. A guitar solo by Jimi Hendrix, or in Henk's lighter moments, Frank Zappa.

Henk was doing heroin, after all.

So when I found myself in roughly the same state Henk had spent most of the seventies, for weeks and months on end in a hospital bed that I couldn't recognise as a hospital bed, little wonder that Henk's story came back to me. If I was doing heroin I might have even believed that it was in fact Henk's old spirit friend in person, come to help me in my time of adversity.

Any friend of Henk's, and so forth.

At the time I didn't have a clue what it was that I was supposed to be recovering from. For all I knew it could have been anything we have come to learn is terminal, from a car accident to a broken heart. My romantic nature tells me that it was a broken heart after all. My eyes would keep swizzle-sticking around at the hospital fluorescent lights and at the blurred faces of my passionate angels; what did I know of what was happening, much less of what had happened?

So I spent all that time with my spirit guide. Or was it Henk's friend, after all?

Meanwhile, my body contemplated whether to live or die. I think my body decided to die. I'm sure there was a time when it was heading off in a wrong direction and Henk's friend caught me and made me stay there in front of the luxurious tapestry, staring at the faces of all the nations of the world.

He was there for me as I floated in a world without pain or memory or music or love. He would take my hand and show me the valleys and reaches of his kingdom. Sometimes too he would taunt me with a little glimpse of what lay underneath, the place that was beyond any emotion we could know in this world, beyond even sadness or lust.

I kept remembering Henk's descriptions of what he saw

under the tapestry. I was full of enough anaesthetic to understand what he had told me.

But in the end of course it was all just a dream, a kind of delayed dream-sharing with Henk, whom I haven't seen for years anyway. When I finally came out of the stupor I was vaguely aware of my dream-friend's absence. The world had moved from summer to winter. Somewhere I'd lost the best part of three seasons, the best part of many other things as well. I made a promise that if I ever ran into Henk, I'd carry him his old friend's regards, even if it was romantic nonsense.

A few days out of hospital and I could walk on my own.

I could see that one day I might even be the person I once was. They gave me my name and told me my memories, yet like a costume designed for another player, a latex mask designed for a more rotund face, these things still seemed a poor fit.

I would go for long excursions around Surry Hills and Darlinghurst, down Oxford Street past Whitlam Square, into the City, down to Rossini's by the Quay. The oddest things would bring me such joy: a waiter serving cappuccino with a stylish Mediterranean swagger, a couple in matching swamp-black tongue-kissing in a doorway, a grey dog. The same things could just as easily bring me to tears. In afternoon film sessions I would be the one laughing, crying. It didn't escape me that I had to get myself back into some kind of perspective.

That's when I met Veronica.

I remember our first conversation had something to do with French movies. Veronica liked to say that they always featured some kind of beautiful but tragic young *grisette* who found solace in a great deal of sexual activity but who usually ended the film by plucking out her eyes or at least forever being lost in the darkness she had been afraid of since childhood. Heavy breasts and a cutaway nightgown incessantly informing the wide screen. We were at opposite poles. But I was already thinking of my dream-friend's rich tapestry when Veronica and I talked. Our second talk had to do with life after death. Veronica is into hydroponic gardens. In Nature, things die and become the blood and bone fertiliser of new life. She thought that maybe human life was the same, our essence nurtures the lives of future generations.

We become Heavenly Manure. It made sense to me.

Some time after that we tried to go and see a French art movie that was advertised with stills of what seemed like a great deal of unsafe sex, but there was another conversation that didn't seem to want to end. We walked around the dark wintry city streets and Veronica showed me the buildings and shops she had known since her childhood. It came to me then that if I were to take Veronica around the buildings and shops of my city, we could do the walk every second week and always see new places or new vacant holes in the earth, and definitely no shops or buildings of my youth; in my hometown, as now with my memory, the concept known as history has seldom been revered.

The movies came up another time.

We actually parked in an expensive station but in front of the Pitt Street Hoyts complex one of us had a change of heart and instead we retrieved the car and visited the beach of Veronica's growing years. She took my hand and showed me the island off Balmoral Beach, the old sandstone steps and little bridge. I dreamed of kissing her in the darkness. I even got her onto the island but a shadowy figure holding a can of beer spooked me and we escaped. We spent the rest of the night at a bar in The Rocks, drinking and abstractedly watching the women's Wimbledon final. With every Crown Lager the fine legs of the players lost their fine focus. I kept smiling at Veronica; I liked the Italian way she used her hands when she spoke to me.

It seemed we were never going to see a movie together or exchange anything but a peck on the cheek. If we wanted more of either, we were going to have to find new partners.

In between the times I saw Veronica, I spent my days walking and looking in shopfront windows as if some jewel or piece of apparel might jump out at me. None did. My legs were getting stronger but my heart was getting weaker. I kept going to afternoon film sessions, I hid my tears behind an arrogant slouch, popcorn, the well-worn sleeve of a seconds leather jacket. At home I looked in the mirror and told myself I was looking better. Veronica never told me how I looked, though she once said I had very long eyelashes.

Then one day when I went to Veronica's place to pick her up for yet another stab at the movies, there was vegetable minestrone on the gas stove and a bottle of chardonnay in the refrigerator. That was the first time I made Benson's acquaintance. Big, neutered, utterly black, scarred, he carried himself with absolute disdain for me. Veronica fed him hand-minced beef, which was the only type of cat food he would eat. No canned nancy-boy gourmet platters for this fading King of Annandale. Benson was castrated late in life and he shouldered the memory of his balls and high times in his swagger and nightly cruise through the neighbourhood streets.

Veronica told me that sometimes when she was dressing, Benson would push open the door of her bedroom with his meaty shoulder in order to sit and watch. She put cayenne on the floor around her door to get him out of his habit.

This alley cat has been around.

So when I sat at the small dining table where Veronica would eventually feed me as well, Benson came and swaggered around my feet three times. I prepared my lap for him and he jumped up. He steadied his bulk against my thighs and stared off into the distance. Machismo glinted from each dark eye. Fresh beef was on his breath. There were scars deep in his fur. I rubbed his back for a long time. He would not acknowledge me but when I put my face to his chest there was the slightest rumble. I bent away and Benson put his face up to mine, whiskers twitching. He is an old fellow. Dribble dripped from his yellow teeth down onto the knee of my jeans. Veronica took to wiping his chin with a tissue. I'm not sure if the kindness was for me or in order to keep Benson from the humiliation of age.

After dinner Veronica put Benson out for his nocturnal ex-cursion and we sat down in front of the television to watch a French film on SBS. When the piano music of Erik Satie started over the titles I kissed her for the first time. It seemed I'd been wanting to kiss those wonderful lips of hers for half my life. I could feel her breath on my face, the touch of her palm. I could see my dream-friend again and he had Veronica's face.

I thought of her as a child on the beach at Balmoral, as a teenager walking around the city shops that were still there, as a woman in the arms of her first lover.

And beneath the tapestry there was the glimmer of the place I wanted to go to. As I kissed Veronica I could feel all the hard months past wanting to come out through my eyes but there was no slouch that could hide me, no popcorn, no well-worn sleeve of a seconds leather jacket. So I kept it back. And in re-turn my dream-friend folded the tapestry back into place.

I have no memory of anything else inside that house.

Out in the cold air and under the full white moon I was almost the person I almost remember from years ago, and it dawned on me to thank God for the fact that it was only an approximation. I think I have been a rich man, I think I have slept in expensive beds with expensive people, I think I have kissed the beautiful faces and secret places of more beautiful and secret people than I will remember—and one of them had almost been my final tragedy. Yet here now with one kiss was a moment beyond love. I looked up at the sky.

Benson was standing by my car. He was looking up at the moon, it was reflected in each iris of his old glassy eyes.

It was good to be back at a beginning.

Henk once told me that his Sioux brothers called this feeling 'jumping at the moon'.

Veronica, I already was.

ABOUT THE AUTHOR

Venero Armanno was born in Brisbane of Sicilian parents and attended the University of Queensland. For ten years after graduation he worked in the computer industry, and travelled throughout Australia and to France, Holland, Switzerland and Turkey. During those years he also wrote fiction, and he has won or been commended in several short story competitions and was shortlisted for the Vogel *Australian* award. In 1991 he completed the scriptwriting course at the Australian Film, Television and Radio School in Sydney. *Jumping at the Moon* is his first collection of stories.

ligature *un*tapped

This print edition published in collaboration with Brio Books,
an imprint of Booktopia Group Ltd

Level 6, 1A Homebush Bay Drive · Rhodes NSW 2138 · Australia

Print ISBN: 9781761282119

briobooks.com.au

brio BOOKS

The paper in this book is FSC® certified.
FSC® promotes environmentally responsible,
socially beneficial and economically viable
management of the world's forests.

MIX
Paper from
responsible sources
FSC® C008194
FSC www.fsc.org